"Are you going to keep laughing?"

"I'm sorry." She fanned herself. "Okay, I'm ready. But you can't expect me not to laugh when you get so engrossed in playing Leonardo."

She walked over to the chair in the corner of the room to use it as a platform to lean against so she could pretend it was the edge of the ship.

She rolled her neck and did a little hop mimicking Aiden when he was preparing to act out a scene. "Okay, let's do this." She leaned against the chair as she glanced behind her to view the scene on the television.

"I changed my mind," he said from behind her. "How about I pretend to be myself instead?"

When did he get so close?

His breath fanned the side of her neck. "Don't come any closer," she said, mimicking the scene. "I mean it. I'll let go."

"No you won't," he whispered in her ear. "I know you, Summer. You can't let go and neither can I."

She sucked in a deep breath at his nearness. "That's not part of the scene."

"I know." He moved to whisper in her other ear. "I'm done acting. Done pretending. At least for tonight. You were right. We're too old to play gar

Dear Reader,

When I was initially creating the Dupree sisters, Summer was the sister I was ready to write about first. Winter, Autumn and Summer are each unique in their own way, but Summer proves that sometimes you have to take a deeper look to understand what someone is going through.

I experienced a range of emotions while writing Summer and Aiden's story. I laughed. I cried. I jumped for joy after writing some scenes, while breathing a sigh of relief for others. I'm a huge fan of friends-turned-to-lovers story lines, so I knew Aiden would be perfect for Summer. They both have experienced disappointments and endured setbacks that have altered their friendship.

Danni's story is next and will release in spring 2017. I can't wait for readers to meet the real Danni Allison. Be prepared for a few surprises you won't see coming!

Much love,

Sherelle

authorsherellegreen@gmail.com

@sherellegreen

Waiting for Summer

Sherelle Green

WITHDRAWN

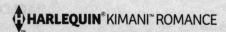

HARLEQUIN® KIMANI™ ROMANCE

Recycling programs
for this product may
not exist in your area.

ISBN-13: 978-0-373-86476-8

Waiting for Summer

Copyright © 2016 by Sherelle Green

Printed in U.S.A.

www.Harlequin.com

Sherelle Green is a Chicago native with a dynamic imagination and a passion for reading and writing. She enjoys composing emotionally driven stories that are steamy and edgy and touch on real-life issues. Her overall goal is to create relatable and fierce heroines who are flawed just like the strong and sexy heroes who fight so hard to win their hearts. There's no such thing as a perfect person...but when you find that person who is perfect for you, the possibilities are endless. Nothing satisfies her more than writing stories filled with compelling love affairs, multifaceted characters and intriguing relationships.

Books by Sherelle Green

Harlequin Kimani Romance

A Tempting Proposal
If Only for Tonight
Red Velvet Kisses
Beautiful Surrender
Enticing Winter
Wrapped in Red with Nana Malone
Falling for Autumn
Waiting for Summer

Visit the Author Profile page at
Harlequin.com for more titles.

To my Godmother who is also my aunt Michelle for being an example of what it means to be a strong, wise and proud woman. Throughout my life, I've watched you in admiration as you overcame any obstacle that life threw your way. Instead of letting obstacles define you, you used that hurdle as a platform to learn from it and walk away with your head held high and a smile on your face. I love the way you enjoy life and the fact that you are always true to your character, never apologizing for being you. What you see is what you get and through you, I learned that being myself is the best person I can be. When I see you, I see an amazing and beautiful woman with a kind heart, infectious spirit and a candid personality that you can't help but love. I feel so blessed to have you in my life and I appreciate you more than you know!

Acknowledgments

To my uncle Ricky—my favorite uncle and the one I can always count on to be there for me. When someone asks me where I developed my love for traveling, I tell them hands down it's because you allowed your nieces to accompany you and your family on trips, giving us an opportunity to explore the world at a young age. You're always there for every member of the family and you're a constant support system to all of us. Being a form of strength and power is something that just comes naturally to you. You love with your whole heart and as a little girl, I used to mirror how you acted because I wanted to be just like my uncle. Thank you for always being a solid rock in my life! I'm not quite sure where I would be without your love and support.

To my aunt Kathy—the aunt who never fails to bring a smile to my face! Growing up, you were always the aunt who I loved to visit. I spent more nights at your house than I can count. Now that I'm an adult, I can honestly say that you're still the aunt I love to talk to when I need a motivating boost or encouraging words. Sometimes, I'm not even sure how you know that I need to hear from you, but it never fails that you seem to contact me at the *perfect* time. Your beauty shines inside and out and being that I love hugs, yours always have a way of warming my heart. Being around you just makes me feel happy and I hope you realize how important you are to me!

Prologue

Two years ago...

"There comes a time in one's life when a crucial decision must be made. Everything worth accomplishing in life starts with being scared. It's okay to be scared, but don't let that fear overpower you."

As Summer Dupree sat in her car staring at the old brown-brick building, she couldn't believe she was chanting words she'd heard from a television program she'd seen last week on people suffering from zoophobia.

Unlike the people on that show, Summer wasn't afraid of animals. She might take off running if a massive and unfamiliar German shepherd ran toward her, but she was a lover of all animals. She rarely saw an animal that unnerved her. Unless that animal walked on two legs and observed her with an intensity that seemed to peel her back layer by layer. Okay, so maybe she was thinking about a human, not an animal. *Well, he's definitely an attractive human.* An *extremely* attractive human.

A human so dangerously sexy that she couldn't think straight sometimes, but that was beside the point.

Movement seen from the corner of her eye got her attention. There was no doubt in her mind that the guy sitting in the car next to her was hyperventilating. Judging by what she could tell from his face, she assumed it was Steve, the class valedictorian. She hadn't talked to Steve that much in high school, but he'd always seemed nice. Within five minutes, she'd already witnessed him remove and wipe his black-framed glasses several times. There was no doubt he was experiencing the same type of anxiety that she was. Then again, was there anyone who didn't experience anxiety attending their high school reunion? She highly doubted it.

With all the courage she could muster, Summer stepped out of her rental and began walking toward the entrance of her old high school. She was wearing her killer red heels and favorite black dress. She definitely looked more confident than she felt. When she reached the door, she exhaled the breath she'd been holding, then stepped into the building.

She barely recalled checking in at the sign-in desk and greeting a couple of former classmates before she began walking down the hall to the gym—a somewhat out-of-body experience. Neither one of her older sisters had returned to town for their high school reunions, yet here she was, walking into the place she swore she'd never step foot in again.

It wasn't that growing up in Claysville, New Jersey, was all bad. There just were parts of the town that she didn't particularly care for. *Like being the main topic of discussion after every town event.* Summer didn't want to blame her hometown for the reason she disliked small towns. But the more she thought about it, the more she wondered if the reason she and her sisters now resided in major cities was because of their experience in Claysville. Both Winter and Autumn were now living in Chicago, and Summer was hoping to move from New York to Miami in a couple years.

The small town of Claysville was only known for three things: its historic buildings, the Fighting Tigers track team and gossip. Summer's family used to live in a beautiful historic home. She had been on the track team, so that was a plus. Unfortunately, her family had also been the main target of gossip, more than any other family in town when they lived there.

When she stepped into the gym, the bright white lights and green and purple balloons representing the school colors transported her back ten years, to her senior prom. She blinked a few times to adjust her eyes to the brightness. Claysville High was the only school she knew that didn't dim the lights for a dance, choosing to keep them bright the entire night. *Unbelievable how some things never change.* Her thought was further proved when Rochelle Slater—the beauty queen herself—approached her.

"Summer, sweetie! I haven't seen you in Claysville since we graduated. How are you?"

Summer returned Rochelle's hug. "Hey, Rochelle, I'm doing well. How are you?"

"Oh, I'm absolutely fantastic. Expecting my second child any day now." She rubbed her protruding belly.

"Congratulations! Is your husband here with you, too?"

"Oh, you silly girl," Rochelle said as she playfully hit Summer's arm. "You call Sam *my husband* as if we didn't all go to school together. I mean, I should really be thanking you."

Here we go. "Thank me for what?"

"Well, we all know Sam had a crush on you through-out grade school and part of high school. If you hadn't shown your true colors, he probably would have never realized that we were really meant to be together." When Rochelle stepped closer, it took all of Summer's energy to remain still.

"You always did want all the men to yourself," Rochelle said in a perky voice, in an attempt to disguise the insult. "Like, all of them. Each and every decent one. So, thank God you released Sam from your grasp so I could snatch him up. I mean, can you imagine if…"

"I think our view on the subject is different," Summer said, cutting her off. "Sam was never mine to begin with. I'm glad you two found happiness."

"Oh, yes, we're very happy. But I haven't forgotten what you put me through with my first boyfriend. In case you were thinking of apologizing for trying to steal Aiden away from me, no need. I accept your apology."

At the mention of Aiden's name, Summer's breath caught in her throat. "Rochelle, I never tried to steal Aiden from you. Aiden and I were only…"

"*Best friends.* Yeah, I know," Rochelle said with a forced laugh. "We've all heard that one before."

"What have we all heard before?" Sam asked as he approached.

Summer briefly looked around the room for an escape. *Okay, where is the black hole? Time travel for one, please!*

"Hi, Sam, how are you?" Summer extended her hand, but their greeting was awkward.

"I'm good. Nice to see you, Summer."

Sam and Rochelle then kissed and embraced. Looks-wise, they hadn't changed much since high school and they genuinely seemed happy to be together. *Hmm, if I liked them more, I'd say they were a cute couple.* But Summer still had the scars from the drama she'd dealt with from them in middle and high school. Against her better judgment, she offered her compliment anyway.

"You both look great together. It's nice to see a couple so in love."

The smile immediately dropped from Rochelle's face. "Is that supposed to be funny?"

"No, it's not. I really mean it," Summer responded in defense. Little did that help, because Rochelle wasn't trying to listen to anything Summer had to say.

"Oh, and I suppose we weren't as cute of a couple before we got Summer's stamp of approval?"

"Uh, what?"

"For your information, the sun does not rise and set on you. Sam and I know what we have and we don't need validation from someone like you."

I'm sorry—what the heck? "I was just trying to be nice."

"I guess some people never grow up," Sam said, comforting Rochelle. "Come on, baby. Let's go talk to some of our other classmates. You can't get upset while you're pregnant."

Summer was sure her mouth was hanging open as they walked away. It didn't matter how nice she tried to be to Rochelle and Sam, they'd already made a conclusion about her character and there was nothing she could do to change it.

Thanks to social media, she still communicated with two of her childhood girlfriends, but neither one of them could make the reunion. She should have listened when they group messaged her not to go. For a ten-year reunion, only about thirty of her seventy classmates had returned, and unfortunately, those who truly knew her weren't in attendance.

"Why the heck did I even come to this shindig?" she said quietly to herself. She knew when it was time to make her exit. There was only one reason she'd come to the reunion. Only one reason she'd decided to throw herself into the line of fire with the couple who'd just walked away.

Although they still talked every now and then, Aiden Chase had once been her best friend. Her biggest supporter. Her trusted confidant. When he'd asked her if she was coming to the reunion, she'd told him that she wasn't going to make it. But although he was usually traveling outside the country for his job as a fashion photographer, he'd informed her that he was attending the reunion even though he didn't want to. Something about needing footage for a documentary being done on him.

It wasn't like her to do surprises, but after some careful thinking, she'd driven back to town in hopes of having her first face-to-face conversation with Aiden in six years. *Maybe we'll finally meet up, like we've been trying to do for a while.* Anything had to be better than staying at the reunion. She wasn't even sure he was still coming.

Summer waved a few goodbyes and stepped out of the building—right into a guy with a camera.

"Sorry, miss. I didn't see you."

"That's okay," she said, before her eyes locked on a couple standing near the end of the parking lot. The couple had their backs to her, but she'd know that guy anywhere. Aiden Chase had finally shown up to the reunion, and by the looks of it, he was still dating the marketing director he'd told her he was no longer with.

Did they get back together? She didn't know what to make of them being together, but he had never lied to her. Aiden Chase was truthful to a fault. The fact that he was also charming and a genuinely nice person meant that people often accepted his brutal honesty.

"Miss? Miss? Did you hear me?"

Summer shook herself out of her daze. "I'm sorry, what did you say?"

"I asked if you went to school with Aiden Chase."

"Yes, I did."

"Great! We're doing a documentary on Aiden and we'd love to capture your interaction with him before he walks into the building."

Oh, my goodness, do they know we used to be best friends?

"How well did you know Mr. Chase?"

Good. Mr. Camera Guy doesn't know. She laughed out of nervousness.

"Fairly well." She left out the part that most of the Claysville population assumed they'd dated in high school.

"Great! Let's have you reconnect with Aiden on camera."

Her heart dropped out of her chest and slammed into the pavement as she listened to the camera guy talk into a walkie-talkie. *Wait! Reconnect with Aiden? On film? In front of a small filming crew and his ex-who-may-not-even-be-his-ex girlfriend?* There was no way that was happening.

Luckily for her, she knew the school better than camera guy did. There was a janitor's closet to the right as soon as you entered the school. She quickly opened the door and slid back into the building. She all but leaped to the closet and twisted the knob.

"Are you kidding me right now?" The door was locked. It was just her luck the school no longer kept it unlocked, like they had years ago.

Summer wasn't surprised when people started gathering in the hallway. It wasn't every day that a camera crew came to Claysville. The front entrance door opened and she immediately knew the crew was looking for her for whatever greeting scene they wanted to portray. She didn't even see Aiden walk in, but she could feel her body heat with awareness. She needed to get out of this hallway, but she knew they would spot her. She looked around for possible exits.

Thank God for small corners. Summer slipped between a locker and the wall, praying that the cameraman who'd spoken to her didn't see her. As the crowd grew larger, the crew quickly forgot about her and took interest in some other possible interactions with Aiden.

Taking advantage of her small escape window, she slipped through the crowd until she'd reached the door again. Just as she was stepping out, she glanced behind her shoulder and saw him. Right there, directly in her line of vision. Their eyes briefly locked and Summer wondered if Aiden would rat her out to his crew but quickly disregarded the irrational thought. She couldn't think such foolishness about the one man in her life who knew more about her than even her own girlfriends.

His eyes cut right through her in a way that made her feel uninhibited. *Man, I miss him.* She'd missed him for a while, but the small glimpse of him made the feeling even more prominent.

His lips curled into a smile as he mouthed the word

hi to her. She returned his silent greeting before slipping completely out the door. She didn't breathe a sigh of relief until she was safely in her car, on the road with the music blasting.

She heard her phone ding indicating a text message. She knew who it was, but waited until she was at a stoplight to briefly glance at the message.

You didn't tell me you were coming. I wish you would have stayed so that we could've caught up. I really miss you, Summer.

She placed her phone back in the cup holder and continued her drive out of town. Oftentimes she thought about how their friendship would be now if things had been different back when they'd walked away from each other. He might have missed her, but she missed so much about him and the friendship they used to have. In fact, she wasn't sure there was anything in the world that she missed more.

Chapter 1

Present day...

If she could pick one superpower in the whole world, there was no doubt in her mind that Summer Dupree would pick the ability to read minds. If she could read her friend's mind right now, she'd know the best way to respond to her question.

"Summer, who's the guy in the photo?" *Or maybe a better choice would be the ability to erase people's memories so that Danni could forget she saw the photo in the first place.*

She glanced over her shoulder at her friend Danni Allison, who had arrived in Miami three weeks ago to help with the opening of the new Bare Sophistication lingerie boutique. The original location in Chicago, Illinois, was thriving under the watchful eye of her sisters, Winter and Autumn. As store manager, Danni had played a major role in the success of their Chicago store; however, Summer was hoping that opening another location in Miami would prove to her sisters that she could further their success. She'd made Miami her permanent home three months ago and had found the perfect Miami Beach location for her boutique. The white brick building had just the right amount of chic and vintage flare.

Although she was confident in her ability to make Bare Sophistication Miami a success, she was glad that Danni had agreed to stay with her until the grand opening the second week of December.

"I don't know who he is. I must have accidentally taken the wrong box out of Winter's storage room." She quickly closed the box and pushed it to the side. "Guess I'll have to ship that box back to Chicago."

"Hmm, you only kept a few things in Winter's storage room and photos weren't in those boxes."

"How do you even know what was in *my* boxes?"

"As manager of Bare Sophistication in Chicago, I had to know everything."

"Or you were being nosey."

Danni scrunched her nose. "When Winter asked me to help her clean her storage room, I may or may not have stumbled upon a few of your boxes. They were already lying open on the floor. And I've seen photos of Winter when she was a little girl. That wasn't her."

Summer shrugged. "Oh, really? Must be Autumn, then."

"Not her, either. Autumn showed me photos of all three of you, so I know it's you in the photo. What's the big deal?"

Summer grabbed the tape from the counter and walked over to the box she'd just pushed away. The boutique was still under construction, so cartons were in an unorganized mess around the wooden floor. Of all the boxes she could have accidentally labeled for the shop instead of her condo, the one containing her photos was the worst one to make that mistake with. Danni was like the female Sherlock Holmes.

"Is he an ex or something? Is that why you won't show me the picture?"

"No, he isn't an ex. Just a friend."

"If he's only a friend, why are you being so secretive?"

After she'd finished taping the box back up, Summer stacked some unopened boxes on top of it. She admired Danni's determination when it came to Bare Sophistication customers. However, in this case, she wished she'd drop it.

"I'm not being secretive. I just prefer not to discuss it."

"Not being secretive?" Danni walked over to Summer and reenacted Summer's reaction to the box when she first opened it. "If you hadn't looked like your hand got caught in the cookie jar, I never would have asked who was in the photo."

Summer was still trying to formulate a response when Nicole LeBlanc and Aaliyah Bai came strolling into the boutique.

"Hey, ladies," Aaliyah said as she glanced around the shop. "Looks like you got a lot done this morning."

"Here you go." Nicole handed Summer a chai tea latte and Danni her usual cup of coffee. "We figured you both would need nourishment for the all-nighter we're about pull."

Summer and Danni only had two months to get the entire boutique ready for the grand opening. Luckily, Aaliyah and Nicole had offered to help. Since Danni had been born in Miami, she knew Nicole from high school. Nicole had been nice enough to meet Summer for lunch when she first arrived in Miami, and they immediately realized they shared a love for fashion and beauty. Nicole was an extremely talented makeup artist and Aaliyah was a beauty photographer who'd met Summer and Nicole at a beauty trade show. The three quickly formed a friendship, which grew even stronger when Danni arrived.

"What did we miss?" Aaliyah asked.

"Nothing much," Danni said as she took a sip of coffee. "Only Summer refusing to tell me about her friend. Her guy friend slash ex-boyfriend. I'm not sure."

"Recent ex-boyfriend or past ex-boyfriend?" Nicole asked.

"Is he cute, average or really attractive?" Aaliyah asked. "Or is he the so-sexy-I-still-see-him-in-my-dreams type of ex?"

Summer cut her eyes at Danni. "How is it that in less than ten minutes you've already started gossip circulating in the office?"

"Girl, please. It's not gossip. I know you were the one in that photo. He looked cute, but I didn't get a good glance. And this is hardly an office. Right now, the boutique is still under construction, and even after renovations are complete, the shop definitely won't have an office feel."

Summer sipped her chai tea latte and started unpacking another box. She didn't want to talk about the photo. She considered all the women in the room friends, but she still didn't feel inclined to be the topic of conversation. Thankfully, they moved on to another conversation and didn't push her any further. This evening, they had to focus on organizing all the boxes, racks and displays, and develop some sort of unpacking system for the next few weeks. The guy in the photo had caused enough distractions to last her a lifetime. Even though Summer had

Danni to help her, she still had a lot on her plate and none of the tasks on her to-do list included thinking about *him*.

Aiden Chase stepped into the building that Palmer Lane Photography was renting for the next year and breathed out a sigh of accomplishment. He'd been a fashion photographer at Palmer Lane for eight years. After having several successful exhibits in Los Angeles and New York, he was finally getting a chance to present his work at Palmer Lane's debut Miami exhibit studio.

"I really like the space you've chosen."

"Thanks," Aiden said to his friend Daxton Perry. Daxton was Aiden's business manager at Palmer Lane Photography. The two had been assigned to work together right after Aiden had joined the company. When Aiden called Daxton and told him he'd found the perfect Miami location for the photo exhibit, Daxton had agreed to fly in from Los Angeles and view the space.

"I got approval to fill out the contract if I agreed that the space was exactly what we were looking for. When we finalize the theme and reach out to the two other photographers, we can start getting everything else into place."

Being one of the top fashion photographers at Palmer Lane had its benefits. Aiden's exhibits in LA and New York had been considerably smaller and he hadn't been the featured photographer in any of his showcases. This Miami showcase was his time to shine. His career was at an all-time high.

"Sounds like a plan. I was hoping you liked the place. Were you able to talk to the team about me residing in Miami for the next six months before I head to Qatar for International Fashion Week in Doha?"

"Yes, they agreed that you should stay in Miami and we'll cover the cost of living and any travel expenses for photo shoots you may have for the duration of your time here. I'll probably travel back and forth to Miami for a couple months, too, until we get the ball rolling."

"Great, because I'm staying at a hotel now, but I already found the place I want to stay temporarily."

"Why am I not surprised," Daxton said with a laugh. "Ever since I approached you with this Miami opportunity, you've been more involved than I've ever seen you for any other project. What are you not telling me?"

Aiden appreciated Daxton's friendship, but he valued his work ethic and keen business sense even more. At thirty-two, Dax was just as driven as he had been at twenty-four when they'd first met. Just last month, he'd been promoted to director of business development; however, he'd agreed to continue being Aiden's business manager since the two had formed a tight bond. Dax was well on his way to becoming vice president of business development for Palmer Lane.

"Nothing to tell. Just excited to be the headline photographer for this exhibit." That was only partially true. Yes, Aiden was excited about the exhibit, but he was even more excited about a certain someone who was opening a boutique a few blocks away from the location of the Palmer Lane exhibit space.

"I have a few calls to make so that we can lock in this property. Do you have dinner plans?" Dax asked as they stepped out the building into the fresh Miami air. It was nearing six o'clock in the evening, so it wasn't as crowded in Miami Beach as it had been midday. Most people were probably getting ready for a night out.

Aiden glanced down the street in the direction of the

one location he'd been thinking about since he'd arrived two days ago. "Umm, I actually do have plans." *Or, at least, I hope I'll have plans.* "How about we meet in the morning?"

"I'm on a red-eye flight tonight, so call me. I'll be at the office." Dax took out his smartphone and was already dialing away as he walked back to his car. Aiden didn't feel like driving back to his hotel. In fact, there was only one place he felt like being and before he could contemplate his next move, his feet were already walking in the opposite direction of his car.

According to Google maps, the address Summer's sister Winter had given him meant that their new shop was only four blocks away. Although he'd briefly seen Summer a couple years ago, when she was leaving their high school reunion, he couldn't believe that he finally had the chance to *really* see her after all this time. There was a time in his life he'd spent every day with Summer. She may not miss him as much as he missed her, but she'd been on his mind a lot lately.

Man, who am I kidding? Summer Dupree hadn't just been on his mind lately. She'd been on his mind constantly since the first day she walked into his kindergarten class.

Twenty-five years ago...

"Class, I'd like you all to meet Summer Dupree. She's new to town, so I want you all to give her a warm welcome."

Aiden looked up from the cartoon picture he was coloring to see the new student. It was a girl. A pretty girl in a pink floral dress.

"Aiden, Summer's going to be your buddy," his teacher said as she walked Summer over to him. "So be nice to her."

"Yes, Mrs. Perkins," he said as Summer took a seat next to him. There were six other students at their table, and until Summer had arrived, he'd been the only one without a buddy since Clarke's family had moved.

"Hi, I'm Aiden." Instead of returning his greeting, she turned to talk to the girls at the table. He was a little disappointed that she didn't want to talk to him, but he kept coloring his picture. A few minutes later, he heard one of the girls asking her to repeat her name. When she did, they snickered a little. Aiden couldn't be sure, but laughing at her name seemed wrong. Though Summer just laughed it off, before long, the whole table was repeating Summer's name and laughing.

Aiden stared at the new girl a little longer. She may be laughing along with them, but her eyes looked sad. He stopped coloring his picture and leaned toward her.

"What's your name again?" he asked. She looked confused.

"Summer." Her voice was really low, as if she assumed he was asking for the same reason the others had. Aiden smiled as big as he could and made sure the other students were listening.

"You have the best name ever! Summer days are the best."

All the other kids began to nod their heads in agreement before returning to coloring their pictures. To his surprise, Summer laughed and leaned over to give him a quick hug. "Thank you, Aiden," she whispered to him.

"You're welcome." Her big round eyes didn't seem sad

anymore and that made him happy. She even scooted her chair closer to him.

"Want to help me color my picture?" Summer asked. Aiden glanced around the table noticing that no other kids were coloring together. When he looked back at Summer, he didn't know why, but he wanted to do anything she wanted to do.

"Yeah, I can help you." They colored for the rest of the time in silence. Usually around this time all Aiden thought about was recess and lunch. Not today. Today was different. Today he was more excited to learn about the girl sitting next to him than he was about anything else.

Chapter 2

"Are we going to take a break and eat soon?" Nicole asked.

"Sure, how about we head down the street to that Cuban restaurant in an hour?" Summer suggested.

"That works," Nicole responded. "There's only so much coffee and tea I can drink. I need food. Or chocolate. Or wine. Hmm, maybe all three."

The women shared a laugh.

"Speaking of chocolate, I almost forgot to tell you guys what I heard," Aaliyah said. "I know we all frequently check out popular magazines for what's hot and new in fashion, so you won't believe who's in Miami right now."

"Who?" Danni asked.

"Well, he's tall and milk chocolate with the type of body that all sex dreams are made of."

Danni huffed. "That could be anybody depending on your type."

"He's also well traveled, under thirty-five and rumor

has it that it's not just his looks that are deadly. He has the personality to match."

"Idris Elba," Nicole guessed.

"She said under thirty-five," Summer said with a laugh.

"Well, he's sexy and chocolate, so Idris is always my first choice. Is it Michael B. Jordan?" Nicole guessed again.

Aaliyah shook her head, indicating that wasn't right, either. "It's someone who works in the fashion industry, but is occasionally in magazines just as much as his work."

Summer froze just as she was picking up another box. Call it intuition, but she didn't think she liked where this conversation was headed. *She didn't say photographer, so maybe it's not him.*

"And he just so happens to be one of the top fashion photographers of today."

The box slipped slightly in her hand when Aaliyah finished her statement. Sure enough, Sherlock Danni was observing her every move.

"Can you nix the details and just tell us who it is?" Nicole asked.

"Aiden Chase," Aaliyah said, clasping her hands together in excitement. "Another photographer I know spotted him walking down the street yesterday."

Summer put on her best poker face as Danni continued to watch her.

"Are you okay, Summer? You look as if you've seen a ghost."

"Yep, I'm fine."

"Really?" Danni walked over to Summer and lifted

the box that kept slipping out of her hands, placing it on the floor. Summer was grateful, until Danni spoke again.

"Aaliyah, I've heard of him before, but what else do you know about him? Since you're a photographer, I know you're more familiar with him than I am."

"I don't know much. Just that he's thirty years old. His work in South Africa is getting a lot of recognition right now. He lives in Los Angeles, but oftentimes, is on the New York fashion scene and he grew up in New Jersey."

"Oh, New Jersey. You don't say?" Danni was speaking to the group, but looking solely at Summer in curiosity. Summer gave Danni her best can-you-please-drop-it? look and, to her surprise, Danni nodded her head in agreement. She then walked over to the sound system they had recently installed and turned the music up a little louder. It didn't matter that Danni had dropped the issue, because now Summer's mind was racing with thoughts about Aiden.

Why didn't he tell me he was coming to Miami? And why didn't he contact me as soon as he got here? Even though they hadn't seen each other in eight years—with the exception of that brief eye lock a couple of years ago—they still remained in contact with each other. He was once her best friend in the whole world. They may have had some disagreements that she'd rather not rehash, but after they'd reconnected via email and social media, it had felt like they were in a good place.

She touched the necklace secured underneath her shirt. They may be in a good place, but they definitely weren't in the best place. Several times, Aiden had asked to Skype or FaceTime with Summer and she'd refused. She hadn't really known why at the time, but after giving it some thought, she'd realized she hadn't been prepared to see him. Even if it wasn't in person.

Growing up in New Jersey hadn't been easy for either one of them. Life after New Jersey hadn't been so peachy, either. Their friendship had always been more of an emotional connection rather than one based on similarities. Although they had a lot in common, they were opposite in a lot of ways, too. In Autumn's words, they complemented each other.

"Are you guys ready to go to dinner now? I think I'm done working for today."

Danni was the first to respond to Summer. "That's fine with me." Aaliyah and Nicole nodded their heads in agreement.

"I'm sorry I was all in your business," Danni whispered to Summer as they prepared to close the shop for the night. "I didn't mean to make you upset."

Summer smiled. "It wasn't you. I got caught up in my own thoughts."

"I understand how that feels. If you ever need someone to talk to, I'm here."

"I know, but thanks for telling me anyway." She'd been thinking about Aiden way more than she should. Regardless of what they'd gone through as friends, her thoughts weren't always so PG-13. Every now and then, he'd say something on the phone or write something in a text message that reminded her that he was—after all—a hot-blooded male. And she was a female who could appreciate all the characteristics that made him irresistible to other women. Not her, but other women for sure.

Just as Summer was locking the door, she felt the hairs on the back of her neck stand on high alert and her breathing grew staggered.

"Oh, my gosh," she heard Aaliyah say behind her. "Isn't that... I think that's..." Her voice trailed off as Summer slowly turned away from the door of the shop toward the person her friends were staring at. She knew who it was before her eyes landed on him.

"Aiden." His name left her lips in a whisper as she gazed at him from across the street. He was wearing a pair of blue jeans that hung on his waist and a deep red V-neck T-shirt that stretched across his chest, accentuating his muscles. Seeing pictures of him on social media or in magazines over the years did nothing to prepare her for actually laying eyes on him in person. Her heart was beating so fast that she couldn't help but clutch her chest to try to slow it down.

There wasn't too much traffic on the street, but enough that he should have been paying more attention to the cars and foot traffic than to her. Yet, even as he crossed the street, his eyes remained fixed on hers. Her gaze briefly left his face to admire his graceful, yet powerful, stride. His walk had always done something to her. He never rushed when he walked, as if he had all the time in the world. She'd never tell him this, but she couldn't even watch him walk without the melodies to every Jill Scott song ever created floating through her mind.

As he approached, she was able to cast her eyes across his face more closely. Aaliyah had described him as milk chocolate, but Summer had to slightly disagree. She'd spent most of her life admiring Aiden's complexion and it was definitely more like a hazelnut dipped in a rich chocolate-caramel blend. His strong jawline, deep gingerbread-colored eyes, and low, neatly trimmed beard took his look from sexy to downright delicious. Not that she was thinking about her friend as delicious. She was just observing a known fact…or so she kept telling herself.

When he finally stood in front of her, he didn't say anything. She felt his eyes on every part of her face, causing her cheeks to grow warmer by the second. *Girl, get a hold of yourself.* This was Aiden. Her old classmate Aiden. Her *good* friend Aiden. He must have sensed her discomfort because he finally broke the silence.

"There are no better days than summer days," he said with a smile, causing Summer to laugh harder than she'd intended. Hearing him say those words brought her back to her first day in kindergarten. She'd laughed then. She laughed now.

"Well, those are the best days," she replied as she leaned up to give him a hug. Just like that, the feeling of discomfort dimmed. It didn't go away, but it definitely lessened. She ignored the butterflies she felt in her stomach when they embraced and, instead, relished the joy of seeing her long-time friend again.

She was there. In the flesh. For once, Summer wasn't a figment of his imagination. She'd even smiled and hugged him, which was more of a greeting than he'd thought he would get. Summer never did like surprises, and Aiden being in Miami was definitely a surprise. He'd expected a playful punch on the arm to be the most contact they'd have.

"How did you get the address to the boutique?" Summer asked. "We don't launch the website until next week."

"Winter gave it to me when I called Bare Sophistication in Chicago."

"Figures," Summer said with a laugh. "What are you doing in Miami?"

"I have an exhibit opening soon, so I'm here to finalize those plans."

"A new exhibit? That's awesome!"

Aiden turned to the woman who had spoken on his left. He'd seen four of them standing near the boutique when he'd crossed the street, but the closer he got, the more his eyes were only drawn to Summer. Judging by the surprised look on Summer's face, she'd forgotten they were there, as well.

"I shouldn't have said anything. The exhibit hasn't been announced yet," he stated.

"No worries, we won't say anything. I'm Aaliyah Bai, by the way."

"Nice to meet you," he said, extending his hand. "I'm Aiden Chase."

"We know who you are," Aaliyah said enthusiastically before winking at Summer. "This is Danni Allison and this is Nicole LeBlanc." Aiden shook both of their hands, as well.

"The four of us were actually going to get dinner at a Cuban restaurant a few doors down," Summer said after the introductions were done. "Would you like to join us?"

Aiden looked from Summer, to the women, and then back to Summer. What he really wanted to do was be alone with Summer, but obviously she didn't want that.

"You know what? I forgot that I need to finish unpacking my stuff back at the condo," Danni said.

"You finished unpacking last week."

Danni ignored Summer's statement and turned to Aaliyah and Nicole. "Ladies, care to join me back at Summer's condo?"

Aiden smiled at Danni's not-so-discreet way of helping him out.

"Summer, why don't you and Aiden go ahead to the restaurant. You can tell us how it is later."

Summer glanced at him before giving Danni a smile that seemed forced. "Okay, then I guess I'll see you when I get home."

Aiden observed her as she watched her friends retreat. She didn't speak after they left, but turned to walk toward the restaurant. As they walked the short distance, she fidgeted with the straps of her purse, taking it on and off her shoulder several times before opting to leave it on her shoulder. Considering how uncomfortable he was making her, he shouldn't have been checking her out—but he couldn't help himself.

"You know, I ate a couple hours ago, so we don't have to eat if you don't want to."

She stopped walking and turned to him. "I could always use a hand lifting some of the heavy boxes in the boutique. The grand opening is in two months, so we're trying to get everything organized since the floors just got done."

Good to know some things haven't changed. When Summer got nervous about something, she always needed to remain busy. As long as she had something else to focus on, she was fine.

"Yeah, that sounds good. I didn't get to the gym or go running today, so I could use a good workout lifting boxes."

She studied his arms and even the simplest look from her warmed his body. "So, you still run?"

"Anytime I can." Running was always something they had in common. "Do you still run?"

"At least four times a week."

His eyes then raked over the snow-white shorts hugging her thighs and her flowy, yellow blouse. When she turned and began walking back to her boutique, he stole a glance at her creamy, butterscotch-colored legs.

He was still staring at her legs when she opened the door to her boutique and motioned for him to step inside.

"Welcome to Bare Sophistication Miami. It isn't much to look at now, but it will be as soon as the furniture gets delivered in a couple weeks. I'm having a lounge space on the raised platform in the corner, and we'll offer tea and infused water throughout the day for our customers."

Aiden observed the space in detail, noting the deep walnut flooring throughout the boutique and crisp white shelving. Lavender, black and gray accent pieces sat on top of random boxes and counters.

"No home for the accent pieces yet?"

"Not yet. When the furniture arrives, I'm hoping I'll lock down the feng shui of this place."

"Well, even though there's still work to be done, I can see the overall look you're going for, and I think it's going to be amazing."

"Thanks," Summer said with a soft smile. "Maybe this will help you visualize the space." She walked over to him and handed him a binder that had been sitting on the front counter.

"Here are some of the preliminary drawings of how everything will look. Still a ways to go, but so far, I'm sticking to my design."

He observed her as she explained each page in the binder, and he couldn't help but listen in pride. She wasn't his girlfriend and never had been. Hell, at the moment they weren't even close friends, more like old friends trying to catch up. Yet the excitement in her smile made him even happier for her.

"Where do these stairs lead to?" He pointed at the staircase in the drawing before turning his head to look at the beautiful wooden staircase.

"There's an upstairs loft area, but I haven't figured out what to utilize the space for yet. I currently have a lot of racks stored up there and the flooring is complete, too."

Summer pulled out a few sheets of paper that were placed in the back of the binder. "And here are a few new designs that Winter is currently working on for the grand opening in a couple months. We will have all the same lingerie as the Chicago location, only we're adding a few pieces to represent that Miami flare. As the boutique matures, we'll add more pieces for our target demographic."

Aiden wasn't sure if the idea for a collaboration popped into his mind because of the way she was explaining the lingerie pieces or because, despite the opening of his exhibit in Miami, the real reason he wanted to be there was for Summer. Or it could be the fact that every lingerie piece she showed him only made him imagine her in it. She was standing so close to him that he could smell her perfume. He couldn't place the scent, but he wanted to bury his nose in the crook of her neck and smell more of it.

"I have an idea."

She looked at him in confusion. "About the lingerie pieces or about the decor of the shop?"

"Both. Neither. I guess both indirectly. I told you that I'm in Miami to feature in the new Palmer Lane Photography exhibit, but I didn't mention that I currently don't have any idea of what the theme of my portion of the exhibit will be. And since I'm the main featured fashion photographer, it has to be a great one."

"I just figured you would be showing photos from some of your many travels. Didn't you just go to Greece not too long ago?"

He quirked an eyebrow at her. "We haven't talked in a while, so I never got to tell you about Greece. Have you been keeping tabs on me?"

She shrugged. "No, but Aaliyah's a huge fan of yours so she keeps all of us updated on the fashion industry."

"I think I just saw some of her beauty shots in *Cosmopolitan* magazine."

She giggled. "You read *Cosmo*?"

"Only because I have to keep abreast of the competition."

"Aaliyah was featured in last month's issue for a contest they had. She's a freelance photographer right now, but she's hoping the *Cosmo* feature leads to more. If you tell her that you spotted her work, she'll probably pass out from excitement."

"So, since Aaliyah is keeping you updated on the fashion industry, when my name got brought up, did you tell her we knew each other?"

She slightly worried her bottom lip, then soothed the bite with her tongue. "Of course I did."

She's lying. They might both be older—and hopefully wiser—but the quirks she'd had when she lied were still the same.

"That's funny, because they looked shocked to see me. I wonder why they all looked so surprised if they already knew we knew each other."

"Hmm, I can't imagine why they were surprised." She

walked over to some small boxes sitting on a built-in shelf and began reading the labels. "So, what's your idea?"

He followed her cue and dropped the subject. "Well, I only arrived in Miami a couple days ago, but I think it's safe to say the fashion in this city is definitely different than what I've seen in other cities. The fashion in Miami is sexy. The colors are bold with heavy Latin influence. The sex appeal in this city alone is enough to make a photographer want to capture the true essence of Miami culture. I'm proud of all my work, but being here makes me want to uncage the fashion culture and represent the true beauty of Miami."

He stepped closer to her. "If the company accepts my idea, I'll call the exhibit *Miami Unleashed* and I'd spend the next few months capturing true Miami fashion. The raw. The weird. The reckless. The sexy."

"I think that's an amazing idea," she said with a killer smile that he hadn't seen in years. Man, how he'd missed that smile. He couldn't even count how many times he'd thought of that smile when he'd been away in a foreign country on a photo assignment.

"What if a few of the lingerie pieces you showed me today were featured in the exhibit? We could set up a photo shoot with models and the works. I could even talk to my business manager about including in your contract for you to be able to hang up pieces in your boutique that aren't chosen to be a part of the exhibit. It only seems fitting that Bare Sophistication be included in *Miami Unleashed*."

It was true that the pieces of lingerie he'd seen would be perfect for the idea that was brewing in his mind. But that wasn't the only reason he wanted to include Bare Sophistication in his idea. There was a time in life when he'd thought he'd always be a friend of Summer's. That there would never be a time when they were apart. He understood that things had happened in their past that couldn't be erased. However, spending eight years feeling like somewhat distant acquaintances rather than the best friends they used to be was more than disappointing. It made him feel empty inside. Alone.

He couldn't quite read the look on Summer's face, but judging from what he could see in her eyes, she was intrigued.

"Would you really be willing to include Bare Sophistication in your exhibit?" she asked.

"Absolutely," he said without hesitation. He still needed approval, but he was sure the folks at Palmer Lane would love his idea.

He was watching her so closely, he was able to pinpoint the exact moment she truly believed in his plan. "Okay, then I think it's a great idea and Bare Sophistication would be honored to be a part of it."

"Great! Let's shake on it until I'm able to have the contract drawn up." He held her eyes as he extended his hand. The minute their hands touched, he felt the same emotions flow through his body that he'd felt when they'd hugged earlier.

"I've been meaning to tell you that I'm sorry the documentary that was being done on you fell through," she said removing her hand from his. "It would have been awesome."

"You told me that via email last year."

"I know, but I wanted to make sure I told you in person."

"Thank you." His eyes dropped to her lips and lingered there for a few seconds.

"Well, then," she said suddenly, as she clasped her hands together. "Now that we've settled the initial awkwardness of catching up, are you ready to help me move some boxes?"

He laughed when she didn't wait for him to respond, but instead, got to work. As they fell into a comfortable silence, Aiden couldn't help but think about how well they worked together on projects in the past. As a matter of fact, he couldn't recall ever working with anyone as well as he'd worked with Summer. They had a lot to talk about and he was sure she'd rather ignore discussing certain topics. However, too much time had passed and too many memories were left unaddressed. He needed her back in his life. Not as an acquaintance. Not as close friend. He wanted her in every capacity.

Chapter 3

Twenty years ago...

Summer ignored the large raindrops falling from the dark sky as she raced across her backyard as fast as she could in her unlaced gym shoes. It was way too late for a nine-year-old to be out, but whenever things got bad at home her best friend was the only one who could calm her down. She felt bad for leaving her sisters at home, but escaping the verbal wrath of their mother was something Summer had gotten really good at the past year.

Her mother, Sonia Dupree, was a piece of work. When Sonia wasn't telling Summer's sister Winter that she wasn't beautiful enough or her sister Autumn that she wasn't smart enough, she was making sure Summer realized that she would never share the close bond that her older sisters shared with each other. She wasn't special, and the sooner she realized it, the better. Winter and Autumn were born eleven months apart, so they were extremely close. Summer only trailed behind Winter by three years and Autumn by two, but sometimes it felt like there were even more years between them.

When she reached her best friend's house, she went behind the shed that was connected to the main house to climb the small rope ladder hanging from the side. When she reached the top, she climbed the short distance to her friend's window and lightly tapped the glass. It wasn't the first time Summer had shown up in the middle of the night in tears after a fight with her mother.

"What happened?" Aiden asked as he helped her inside and wrapped a blanket around her.

"My mom is arguing with my sisters again and my dad won't be home from his work trip until tomorrow. They are only fighting with her because of me. It's all my fault."

In between her sobs, Summer explained that her mother had arrived home looking to pick a fight with her daughters. Tonight, Summer was the object of her wrath because she had told her mother that she was only watching television because she had finished her homework early. Summer knew better. She wished she had cut off the television as soon as she heard the key turn in the front door indicating Sonia was home.

The yelling had quickly escalated when Summer couldn't find the remote fast enough to cut off the program. Despite the fact that her mother initially began arguing with her, Winter and Autumn deflected the argument so that Sonia wouldn't continue to yell at Summer. Of course, that only made Sonia angrier, and as soon as she caught on to the deflection, her wrath turned back to Summer.

"Your sisters can handle it," Aiden said as he cut on a

lamp and sat with Summer on the floor. "You know how your mom gets. All the yelling will wear her out soon."

"I just don't understand why she's like this. Why can't she be like the other moms and give us hugs and tell us that she loves us? All she does is yell and tell us how much she hates that we were ever born."

"Everyone isn't meant to be a parent. Don't give her that power and let her upset you. She isn't worth it."

Summer glanced at Aiden with tear-streaked cheeks and instantly began to feel better. "You know, if we weren't in the same grade I'd swear you were a grown-up." Aiden wasn't only mature for his age, he towered over most of the boys in their grade.

Aiden laughed and began imitating their fourth grade teacher who was constantly telling him he needed to act his age. But that was Aiden. Nine going on twenty-nine. Her dad, Vail Dupree, always said that Aiden was an old soul trapped in a young body.

"Thanks for making me laugh," Summer said when her laughter began to die down. "You always make me feel better."

"That's my job as your best friend." Aiden stood and walked over to his dresser. "I've been saving my allowance all year to get you this gift. I was going to wait until Christmas in a few months, but maybe you should have it now."

She opened the small white box he handed her and gasped when she noticed a gold locket that had *Best Friends* engraved on it. When she opened the locket, she found a picture of the two of them at summer camp a couple of months ago on one side and her sisters on the other.

"How did you have enough money to buy this?" Her eyes grew wide. "Unless you didn't buy it."

"Relax, Dupree. I didn't steal it," Aiden said with a smile. "My dad gave me a couple months' allowance early so that I could get it before the store sold out. Do you like it?"

"I more than like it. I love it. How could I not love it when you included pictures of my three favorite people?" She didn't feel a need to say that of the three, Aiden was her most favorite.

"Every time you feel like you're alone and need to escape, look at this locket and know that I'm right there with you."

She studied the locket a little more before she glanced at Aiden. "It's the best gift I've ever gotten."

His mouth curled to the side in a crooked smile that she was starting to like more and more each day. Even though he'd always be Aiden, her friend who happened to be a boy, she was starting to see why so many girls had a crush on him. Ever since Rochelle Slater told all the girls during summer camp that she knew Aiden liked her because he would always give her a special side smile. Summer had then wondered why Aiden gave her the same smile if that's what he gave the girls he liked.

"I'm glad you like it." He playfully shoved her shoulder. "Just remember around Christmastime that I gave you your gift early."

"I won't forget." She handed him the locket to clasp around her neck. "I have to go back home, but I'll see you tomorrow at school."

She gave Aiden one last hug before tying up her shoes and climbing out the window. The rain had slowed down, so it wasn't as slippery outside as it was when she had left her house.

Once she reached the end of Aiden's driveway, she waved goodbye and tucked her locket into her shirt before running home. Running was quickly becoming one of her favorite things to do. Not only did running help her get away from her mother, but when she ran, she felt free. Alive. As if everything in the world would be okay. Running helped her clear her mind and made her remember that despite the fact that her mom didn't really love her, she still had her dad and her sisters. She didn't know what she'd do without them. *Or Aiden*, she thought. She didn't know what she'd do without him, either.

Present Day...

Every time you feel like you're alone and need to escape, look at this locket and know that I'm right there with you. Summer thought about the words that were voiced to her nearly twenty years ago. Words that had offered her comfort in a time of need. Throughout the years, every time she'd felt alone or needed an escape, his soothing voice would drift into her mind.

She probably shouldn't wear her locket while she jogged. Anything could happen to it and she cherished it more than any other piece of jewelry she owned. However, she felt naked when she wasn't wearing it. Like a piece of her was missing.

Glancing at her Fitbit, she realized she'd already been jogging for over an hour and the sun was starting to set. She needed to head back to her condo if she was going to get any unpacking accomplished today. Three months there and she still hadn't fully unpacked her kitchen or bedroom.

As soon as she arrived back home, she kicked off her sandy gym shoes and walked into her bedroom. She covered her ears from the blast of music that shot through her walls.

"I swear this place has the thinnest drywall known to man," she shouted to herself. It never failed that every Tuesday, Thursday and Sunday, Summer's neighbor would blast music as loudly as he could. On Sundays he played orchestra music, Thursdays he played soundtracks from musicals, and on Tuesdays—her least favorite day—he cranked up the opera.

Danni had decided to go to a Zumba class with Nicole and Aaliyah. Summer hadn't gone with them in hopes of having some time to herself after her run. But with the opera music so loud, there was no way she would be getting any R & R.

"Mr. Higgins, can you please turn it down," she yelled as she banged on her wall. She knew he could hear her. When she'd first moved into her condo, he'd startled her when he'd knocked on the wall and answered a question that she'd asked herself. Her complex was located in between downtown Miami and Miami Beach. It was supposedly one of the best, which was why she was thrilled when she'd seen the reasonable price of her place.

She'd missed the unstated disclaimer that having a top-floor apartment in the corner came with thin walls and an inconsiderate neighbor. There were only three condos in her wing of the building. When she was told that one condo was occupied by a professional dancer who often traveled and the other was occupied by a seventy-five-year-old man, she didn't think she'd have to worry about music being played too loudly.

When he didn't respond to her second knock, she went into the hallway to knock on his actual door. The music stopped for a couple seconds, so she used the silence to her advantage. "Mr. Higgins, it's Summer Dupree. I know we haven't personally met, but I'm your neighbor. Can you please turn down the music a little?"

She waited for a minute with no response from her neighbor. Just as she was walking away, she heard the door crack open.

"Mr. Higgins?"

"What do you want?"

She swallowed back a gasp at the harshness in his voice. He'd only opened the door about a couple centimeters wide. "I was wondering if you could turn down the music."

"No."

Summer blinked a few times. "No? Not at all? I wanted to ask you before I called management."

She'd barely gotten out all her words before he began laughing at her. "Foolish girl, you'll do no such thing. I've been living here for over thirty years. That's probably longer than you've been alive."

"I understand that," she said trying to remain reasonable. "But my bedroom and bathroom share a wall with your condo, so every time you play the music that loud, the picture frames in my bedroom shake and things fall out of my bathroom cabinet. A few of my accent pieces have even broken from falling off my dresser."

"Superglue and permanent adhesive."

"What does that mean?"

He groaned in frustration. "Superglue and permanent adhesive." He said it slower as if it would suddenly make sense to her.

"Maybe I should just call management." She was about to head back to her condo before he explained himself.

"I suggest you buy some superglue and adhesive to stick all of your important belongings to your dresser so that they won't fall."

"Excuse me?" *Who was this guy?* If he weren't so rude, she'd compliment him on his voice. The words he spoke were normal, but the tone of his voice sounded as if he'd walked out of a Shakespearean play.

"And while you're shopping for glue and adhesive, you should get a better cabinet, too. I've known current management since they were babies in diapers. Family-owned business. If you need their number, you can find it on the bulletin board of the first-floor foyer. I also ask that you refrain from knocking on my walls and door for the rest of the night. It disrupts my euphoria when I'm listening to my music."

The door slammed in her face before she could say anything else. "Unbelievable." She walked back to her condo even more annoyed than she had been before she'd knocked on Mr. Higgins's door. She'd only met her other neighbor once. The dancer had claimed that Mr. Higgins was a piece of work, but had assured Summer that he'd grow on her.

"Ha!" It was hard for him to grow on her when she could barely hear herself think. She contemplated heading to her boutique to get some work done there, instead. After showing Aiden the idea she'd had for the boutique a couple of days ago, she'd gotten even more fired up to turn her decor visions into a reality.

She sat in her plush round chair next to her bedroom window overlooking the beautiful city of Miami. She needed to hop in the shower, but she couldn't stop her brain from going a mile a minute. Summer had always handled stress well, but as of late, she couldn't seem to stop her brain from overthinking everything she had to do. Usually she compartmentalized her feelings into categories so that she could tackle one issue or area at a time.

Out of the corner of her eye, she caught sight of her lavender notebook and favorite ballpoint pen. She'd often used them to jot down her thoughts back when she was living in New York.

She'd enjoyed her career working at a top fashion public relations firm. The firm had allowed her to split her time between their New York and Miami offices. However, she'd known it was time to move on and pursue her ultimate dream of opening up a Bare Sophistication lingerie boutique in Miami.

Aiden...

Her mind drifted to him, as it often did. With his current company having a New York office and her previous company being in New York, she found it surprising that with the exception of that random reunion moment, the only time their paths had crossed was a couple of days ago. *Not that surprising, since you were the reason he kept his distance.*

Just as she began jotting down decor ideas for the boutique, her iPhone rang.

"Hey, Danni, is everything okay?"

"Everything's fine. Zumba was great, but Aaliyah was in a bad mood throughout most of the class. After the workout, we went out for veggie and fruit smoothies and she told Nicole and me that she just lost a big client."

"Please tell me it's not the cosmetics company she was excited about. The one with the new organic makeup releasing in two months who wanted her to capture photos of the entire line for their website."

"That's the one," Danni said with a sigh. "She's really disappointed so I wanted to see if we had a few hours tomorrow night to spare to take her out and hopefully cheer her up."

"I think that's a great idea. We can always spare time for her."

"Thanks, Summer! I'll let the girls know."

Summer was still thinking about Aaliyah minutes after she disconnected the call. All of them were in the fashion and beauty industry and even though they had established careers, each of their careers was still a work in progress and ever evolving. Their work wasn't easy, and every day Summer thought about how she could highlight her friends' talents in Bare Sophistication instead of just utilizing their help with getting the shop ready for the grand opening.

Without focusing too much on what she was drawing or writing, Summer began to let her pen flow across the current page of her notebook. She thought about the Chicago lingerie boutique and the unique way her sisters tapped into the bachelorette and bridal business by incorporating masquerade lingerie parties into the boutique's services. She then thought about Aiden's idea to feature Bare Sophistication in his photography exhibit to represent the sexiness of Miami—and the exposure they would receive if everything went as planned.

Rubbing her locket with her left hand, she let her right hand do most of the work, further thinking about the beauty trade shows she'd attended throughout the years.

She leaned over to her small bookcase and pulled out her tablet to view the details she had regarding her budget and photos of the layout of her shop. It wasn't until her hand stopped moving that she noticed the music on the opposite side of her bedroom wall had actually gotten louder than it was before.

She stared at the wall as if it were a mirror staring back at her. Glancing back down at her notebook, she looked at the preliminary plan she'd present to the girls tomorrow.

There was no guarantee that they would be interested in her plan, but if they were, there was no doubt in her mind that Bare Sophistication Miami had just found its niche in the industry. "Well, well, you crazy old man. Guess your opera music served me well tonight."

Chapter 4

"Thanks for the detailed email yesterday," Daxton said on the other end of the phone. "I presented your idea to the CEO and the rest of the team and they loved the idea of *Miami Unleashed* for your feature exhibit."

Aiden raised his fist in victory as he peered out of the floor-to-ceiling window in the penthouse suite of the hotel he was staying at. It had been three days since he'd seen Summer and he couldn't wait to tell her the news. "I was hoping you'd say that. And I have complete creative freedom?"

"Yes, you do. I just need you to keep me abreast of your plan of action because we're already working on concepts for the other two photographers being showcased."

"I'll make sure I keep you in the loop, but just like I wrote in the email, the overall idea is to represent the sexiness of Miami. I want to show the raw fashion. The somewhat unorthodox fashion. The fashion that may lie beneath the clothing. A lot of folks don't look at Miami as a fashion capital like LA and New York, so I want to change their view through my photos. Which is why a few pieces will be photos of Bare Sophistication's lingerie collection."

"I meant to ask you about that." Aiden could hear Dax typing on his laptop. "I did some research and although Bare Sophistication has a location in Chicago, the Miami one hasn't opened yet. How did you hear about this place and why will it be a central part of your exhibit?"

Aiden cleared his throat. "You've never asked me details about my work before."

"Well, we've never given you complete creative control before. You're already one of our top fashion photographers and even though you travel out of the country for us a lot, you said your next move is nailing a high-profile corporate position. You want to be the creative director of our travel and fashion photographers in our London office. That's a huge responsibility."

"I know it is, but after eight years of being a fashion photographer for Palmer Lane, I'm ready to step into a new role. Besides, now that Palmer Lane has partnered with Rogan Studios, the idea of merging film and photo is too good to pass up." *And it puts me one step closer to fulfilling my dream of filming a documentary.*

"I'm sure the London partnership will stream down to the other offices within the next two years. So why not get more involved in the New York office like you are in LA? They've wanted you in New York permanently for a while now, since the fashion scene is larger. You're traveling to New York all the time anyway, and eventually my new role will place me there permanently."

Aiden ran his fingers across his face. "Living in Jersey, I basically grew up in New York. LA was a nice change, but London will be even better."

The line grew silent. "Dax, are you still there?"

"Yeah, I'm here. Look, as your business manager, I have to question you more than usual about this exhibit because you're up against some stiff competition. But as your friend, I have to ask you if this is really what you want."

They'd talked about it before, so Aiden knew where the conversation was headed.

"Yes, I want the position."

"Okay, man, if you want it, then I want you to have that position just as much as you do. I just always thought that, by now, you'd have moved on from Palmer Lane."

"You haven't moved on."

"I'm in sales. You're on the creative side. Our worlds are completely different and I know you've been approached with opportunities from other companies. Photographers with your talent usually don't do the same thing for too long. I won't go there with you right now, but don't think I don't notice things."

Aiden opened the sliding door and stepped out onto the balcony. "And what things do you notice?"

"Well, for starters, did you honestly think I wouldn't find out that Summer Dupree is the owner of the new Bare Sophistication store that's opening soon? The same company that happens to be the main inspiration for your exhibit?"

Aiden laughed. "So you do remember when I told you about her."

"Man, you date even less than I do, and that's saying a lot because I rarely have time to date. Summer is the only woman you've ever mentioned to me."

"What about Adriana? You actually met Adriana and we dated for two and a half years."

"You mean the Adriana who left the Palmer Lane office throwing vases at my head even though you're the one who'd just broken up with her? That Adriana?"

"Any grown woman who throws a temper tantrum in a public place has a lot of growing to do. You should have seen my office."

"Childish or not, she never stood a chance with you. You're one of the most down-to-earth guys I know, but around her, you weren't yourself. You were closed off. I'm not even sure she truly knew you."

Aiden thought about Daxton's words. Adriana hadn't expected the breakup, but he knew it had been the right thing to do. "It wasn't fair to date her for as long as I did. I know that now."

"My sister tells me that all men are slow, so don't blame yourself. Our gender never had a chance at easy breakups. Have you seen Summer yet?"

"I saw her a few days ago at her boutique and I helped her organize a few heavy boxes."

"That's good. Hopefully, you can rekindle your friendship with her. I know she means a lot to you."

Means a lot was an understatement, but Dax didn't need to know all that. "Thanks, man. If I think of any additional details for the creative portion of the exhibit, I'll email you later today."

"Sounds good."

After disconnecting his call, Aiden stretched his arms before leaning over the balcony to view the red-orange sun setting over beautiful Biscayne Bay. Although the view was fantastic, Aiden had stayed in enough hotels to last a lifetime. He'd contact the realty company for the temporary home he wanted soon.

Movement in his peripheral caught his eye. There was

a couple a few balconies over who'd clearly had a much better morning than he had. Not that his morning had been unpleasant. But judging from the looks on the man's and woman's faces, their morning had included some extracurricular activities.

He thought back to his conversation with Dax about Adriana. A year after they'd broken up, she'd apparently found someone else and had called him to let him know that she now knew what true love felt like. He'd told her he was happy for her, and her response had been that he should really figure out what or who was blocking his heart. She'd claimed he only shared a part of himself with her, but she always knew he had more to give. He hadn't said anything to her at the time, but instead, he'd remained silent while she hashed out her feelings. Feelings that he was all too familiar with. She'd said that, at times, it seemed like he didn't really care about her at all. That wasn't true. He had cared about her, even if his heart had been blocked. He told her such, but she didn't seem to listen. He didn't push the issue because, unfortunately, she wasn't the first woman to tell him that.

Seventeen years ago...

"I'm so excited we're here," Rochelle said with a squeal when they walked into the dance. Aiden only smiled and tried his best not to get annoyed by the way she was tugging on his arms.

"It's the last dance we'll have before high school starts. Aren't you excited Aiden?"

"Thrilled." He hoped his voice didn't sound as nonchalant as he really felt.

"Why can't you at least pretend to be happy that you're at the dance with me?"

"I am happy to be at the dance with you."

She crossed her arms over her chest. "Then why are you looking around the room like you're trying to find someone else? You better not be looking for Summer."

"Why can't I look for Summer? Aren't you going to look for your friends?"

"My friends are all girls. No boy and girl should be best friends. It doesn't make sense."

He sighed. "I have guy friends, too, so how about you look for your friends and I'll look for my friends."

When he stopped looking around the room for Summer and looked at Rochelle, he noticed how sad she looked.

"I'm sorry," he said sincerely. "Do you want to dance now and we'll find our friends later?"

"Yes," she said with a big smile, before grabbing his hand and leading him to the dance floor. He really did like Rochelle, but he didn't understand why she always got so upset about Summer. They were just friends.

"This is nice," Rochelle said when they were on their eighth song. Aiden discreetly looked around the room as she talked. *Summer should be here already.* Last time he'd talked to her, they'd agreed to arrive with their dates around the same time.

"Yeah, it's nice." Aiden spun them around so that he could look at the other side of the room. Still no Summer. "Rochelle, I have to go to the bathroom. Why don't you find your friends until I return?"

She only looked skeptical for a moment. "Okay, but hurry back. There's only an hour left of the dance."

As soon as Aiden stepped out of the gym, he glanced

down the hallway before stepping outside to look for Summer. Just as he'd suspected, he found her by her favorite oak tree in the school's front yard.

"Hey, pretty girl. What are you doing out here?" He sat down in the grass beside her and noticed her eyes were watery. "What happened? Why are you crying?"

She sniffled before wiping her eyes. "Remember that blue dress Winter made for me?"

"Of course. You looked beautiful in it." Only then did he notice she was wearing one of her old dresses.

"I guess I looked too beautiful in it, because when I got home from school today, I saw it in pieces. My mom told me that she needed to make herself a new outfit and needed the material Winter had used for my dress."

Aiden shook his head in annoyance before pulling Summer closer to him. "Where are your dad and sisters?"

"My dad was arguing with my mom about it and I left the house with Autumn and Winter. They walked me to the dance and I waited until they left before I walked back out here. I can't walk into the dance in this dress. I've worn it so many times before and I don't want Sam to see me in it again."

"If Sam really likes you, he won't care what type of dress you're wearing." He brushed her hair out of her face. "Your mom is always doing something mean and you usually never care what people think. Are you crying because you don't want Sam to see you in this dress or because of something else?"

"Guess I'm not good at hiding my feelings, huh?"

"Maybe to some people you are, but I pay more attention to you than most people. So what's really wrong?"

Summer pulled out a folded piece of paper from her jacket and handed it to him. "I didn't come straight out here. I went to my locker to get my blue jean jacket to try to hide the fact that I'm wearing this dress again, and I found this."

As Aiden unfolded the paper and started reading the letter she'd received, he got more pissed off by the second.

"Who wrote this?"

"If I knew who wrote it, I'd confront them."

The letter was making fun of Summer's friendship with Aiden. It called her a pathetic loser who couldn't get a girl for a best friend, so she had to get a boy to pretend to like her enough to be her best friend. However, Aiden knew that wasn't the part that had Summer leaning against the tree crying. The letter also had cartoon illustrations of a woman wearing tight clothes surrounded by a bunch of men and her three daughters watching from afar. The illustrations continued on the back page.

Everyone in the small town that they'd grown up in knew of Sonia Dupree, and her infidelity wasn't exactly a well-kept secret. More like town gossip.

"I'll figure out who wrote it." Just as Aiden was balling up the letter, he studied the way the words were illustrated instead of written normally. Then he focused on the drawings themselves. There were only a few people in their grade who were talented enough to draw cartoons like that and he was one of them.

"I know who drew this." Aiden stood and marched back into the school with Summer hot on his tail.

"Aiden, would you slow down? Where are you going?"

He didn't listen to her and continued to walk at a fast pace until he reached the person he was looking for.

"I know you did it, Sam," Aiden said grabbing his shoulder and turning him around. "You put that letter in

Summer's locker. You owe her an apology, so either you give it to her or I'll make you apologize."

"I don't know what you're talking about," Sam said with a smug smile. "I've been waiting at this dance for Summer for two hours, so if anyone needs to apologize, it's Summer to me."

"She doesn't owe you anything."

"Oh, yeah?" Sam stepped closer to Aiden. They were around the same build, but Aiden was an inch taller. "I don't owe her anything and I heard my dad talking to his friends about her mom. Doesn't her mom have enough men in her life without going after my dad? With a mother like hers, I don't know what I was thinking asking her to this dance anyway. And judging by the way she follows behind you, like mother like daughter."

Aiden had always been taught that violence wasn't the answer, but at the moment, he didn't care. He'd never been in a fight before. He'd never even felt an urge to punch someone before now since he was friends with most of the guys in their class.

None of that mattered the longer he listened to Sam criticize Summer. His fist connected with Sam's face faster than he could process what he was doing. Before he knew it, they were in a brawl on the dance floor with Aiden on the winning side. He wasn't sure how long they would have continued fighting if one of the teachers hadn't broken up the fight.

When he finally looked over at Summer, he could tell she wasn't too happy with him.

"Aiden Patrick Chase, did I ask you to fight my fight for me?" She didn't give him a chance to respond. Sam was barely off the ground before Summer walked over and punched him square in the face. She shook the hurt out of her hand and smiled at Aiden before giving him a wink. That was Summer. Her relationship with her mother may have been one of her emotional triggers, but Summer never let anyone walk over her. Amid the chaos, he heard someone crying.

"Are you okay?" he asked Rochelle.

"Did you think about the fact that you would be ruining the end of our last eighth-grade dance before you hit Sam?"

"He said some really cruel things to Summer."

"I heard some of the argument so I know that, and I'm sorry he hurt her feelings. But what about my feelings? Why did you even ask me to this dance? I could have gone with someone who actually likes me."

"I do like you." He didn't get a chance to explain because Rochelle left the gym just as the teacher who broke up the fight approached him. Sam hadn't really been hurt, but both he and Summer were told that they would be suspended for a week and couldn't walk in the eighth grade graduation.

His dad was extremely disappointed when he picked him up after the dance and asked him if he regretted what he'd done. Aiden chose not to respond at the time. He knew fighting was never the answer and he would apologize to Sam at school the next Monday. However, if given the choice to redo the night, there was nothing he would have done differently. He could handle people making fun of him, but he couldn't handle seeing Summer hurt from getting teased about her mom.

Summer was right. She didn't need him to fight her battles. Still, what type of best friend would he be if he didn't stand up for her and fight alongside her every once in a while?

Chapter 5

Summer glanced at her phone to check the time and to see if Aaliyah or Nicole had texted to say they were running late. She'd contacted the girls three hours earlier and asked if they could meet her at the reggae lounge two hours before the live music would begin so that she could discuss a business proposition with them.

"Can I get a hint about what you want to talk to us about?"

Summer looked up from her phone at Danni. "Nope," she said with a smile. "I want it to be a surprise. You guys may not even like the plan, and if you don't, my feelings won't be hurt."

"So, this really is about business? Not a certain someone who I'm not going to even mention because I don't want to seem nosey?"

Summer's face dropped. "Seriously? That wasn't even the least bit discreet."

"I wasn't going for discreet. I was shooting for blatant."

"Oh, yes, Danni, that makes all the difference," Summer said sarcastically. "Unfortunately, Aaliyah and Nicole are here so we'll have to continue this conversation later." Danni was still giving her the side eye when the ladies approached.

"Thanks so much for meeting me early," Summer said as they took their seats.

"No problem," Nicole said, as she laid her clutch on the table. "What did you want to talk to us about?"

Summer looked in her bag and pulled out her tablet and lavender notebook. "When Danni called and told me about Aaliyah losing her client, it got my brain to working."

She went through the photos in her tablet until she found pictures of the loft area of her boutique. "Nicole and Aaliyah, ever since I met you both, I've been trying to think of a way for Danni and I to collaborate with each of you. If you look at these pictures of the loft, you may notice that the room gets a lot of sunlight. The company that occupied the space before me had the loft remodeled to include a separate room and bathroom as well as other section dividers. I assume it was to split up the space, which is perfect for my idea."

She opened her lavender notebook to make sure she didn't miss anything as she spoke. "Danni is a business and management whiz. I have expertise in fashion PR, marketing and graphic design. Nicole, you're an amazing makeup artist and hairstylist, although you rarely talk about your awesome styling ability. And Aaliyah, you're a fantastic beauty photographer who has done a variety of work in Miami and other cities. Together, the four of us have pretty amazing skills."

She pulled out the photos she'd stuffed in her notebook. "Aaliyah, I remember you telling Nicole and I about some work you used to do."

"Aww, did you Google me to get these pics?" Aaliyah asked, as she admired some of her previous work.

"I did," Summer said with a laugh. "And I'm happy to say that I've finally figured out what to do with the upstairs loft of the boutique. I want to turn that section into a boudoir studio. Women would not only be able to purchase lingerie from our first-level boutique, they would also be able to book a boudoir photo shoot. We will do their hair and makeup, style them with accessories to complement the lingerie they purchase, and offer them photo packages. Aaliyah, I had no idea you had so much experience with boudoir photos."

"I do, and it's one of my favorite types of work. There's nothing better than making women feel sexy."

"I agree! All four of our skill sets would be needed to make this a success. But since the sign on the outside of the boutique just says Bare Sophistication, we can add to that."

"What would you add?" Danni asked excitedly.

Summer scrunched her forehead in thought. "Bare Sophistication Boutique and Studio for the sign, but we'll have a motto, of course. Something like, *Bare Sophistication...capturing your beauty inside and out.* Or maybe something like *Empowering the everyday woman.* Danni, we could work together to come up with something great, and when you go back to Chicago maybe you could see if something like this could work in that location, as well. I just want to give women a place where they can let their hair down and really tap into their sensuality. When Winter, Autumn and I initially came up with the idea for Bare Sophistication, we always wanted the boutique to be a place where women of all shapes, sizes and nationalities could come and feel beautiful. Inspired. Confident."

The women each wore smiles, but no one said anything. Summer started getting nervous that they didn't like the idea even though they seemed pleased. "We all work so hard and I thought it may be nice to combine forces. I know there's more to work out and it wouldn't be a full-time thing. Only when we have boudoir clients. What do you guys think? Danni's already going to be on the Bare Sophistication Miami website, but I could add you both, as well. Profiles, pictures, bio…the whole shebang."

"Summer Dupree," Danni said, shaking her head. "You are a genius. I love this idea!"

"You do?" Summer asked clapping her hands. "I was hoping you liked it."

"She isn't the only one." Aaliyah leaned over to hug Summer. "I was feeling out of sorts after I lost my client. Especially when they didn't give me a viable reason why they didn't want to utilize my photography skills. I'm definitely down for being a part of Bare Sophistication's boudoir studio. Not only is the message one that will resonate with women everywhere, but I think we just figured out why we all came into each other's lives."

"I'm in, too," Nicole said cheerfully. "I was already fine with helping you with the boutique, but now I have even more invested. I have a feeling we're onto something great."

Summer finally relaxed and released the nervous breath she'd been holding since she'd arrived at the lounge.

"So, now that we've covered the business portion

of the night, can we talk about how you know Aiden Chase?" Aaliyah asked.

Danni raised her hands in the air. "Finally, someone asks besides me. I've been dropping hints for the past few days and Summer hasn't said a peep."

Nicole ordered a cocktail from the waitress before jumping into the conversation. "Yeah, I'm dying to know the story, too."

Summer sighed as she fidgeted with her notebook. With the exception of her sisters, who treated Aiden like a little brother, she couldn't recall the last time she'd had to talk about him to anyone. *That's because you never talk about the things that are close to your heart.* When it came to meeting new people, Summer was a social butterfly. When talking about business, Summer could go on for hours. Those who just knew her on the surface would have said she was an open book. Yet, the truth was, whether bad or good things, Summer was private about more than a few aspects of her life.

"Aiden and I grew up together in Jersey, so I knew Aiden Chase before he was *the* Aiden Chase."

Danni nodded her head in understanding. "And he was in that picture you boxed back up, wasn't he?"

"Yeah, it was a picture from when we were in high school."

"So, did you guys date?" Nicole asked.

"No, we never dated. We were best friends growing up, so it wasn't like that."

The ladies shared a look that didn't go unseen by Summer. "What's that look about?"

"Of course we have to take your word for it that you never dated," Aaliyah said. "But the way he was looking at you wasn't in a best friend sort of way."

Summer's cheeks warmed immediately at Aaliyah's words. Since Summer and Aiden were of opposite sexes, they'd been teased most of their friendship. She was sure most of the people in their hometown wouldn't even believe they had never actually dated.

"Well, I guess, in a way, we were always more than friends. But not in the way that you'd think. We didn't really have the easiest time when we were growing up, so I guess you could say we were each other's security blanket."

She glanced at Danni, who gave her a sympathetic smile. Even though Summer hadn't talked to Danni about her mother, she knew Winter and Autumn had told her a few things.

"We all need someone like that in our lives," Danni said. "I'm glad you had him to lean on."

"Me, too." Her eyes drifted to the dance floor as she smiled at a memory of herself and Aiden. "Being as close as we were, for as long as we were, never seemed strange to me. Looking back, I see how confusing it must have been for the people we dated."

Nicole laughed. "How long have you known each other?"

"Oh, goodness. We met in kindergarten and immediately became friends."

"Wow, that's a long time. I don't think I know anyone from kindergarten."

"My family had just moved to the area and Aiden was one of the first kids I met. Since he was a boy and boys had cooties back then, I didn't pay him much attention in the beginning, but we eventually bonded over coloring. When it was time for lunch and everyone pulled out their lunch boxes, all the kids would talk about how much they love ham-and-cheese sandwiches. Aiden and I both said we hated ham at the same time. According to him, he knew we would be friends when we first started coloring together, but that was the moment he knew we were meant to be best friends."

She thought about the way the other students had looked at them that day. They'd spent the rest of that afternoon together and every day after that. They both had other friends, but none of their friendships were as close as the one they shared.

"The first few years of school were a breeze in regard to our friendship. By the time we hit middle school, things weren't so easy."

"Don't girls and boys start actually liking the opposite sex by then?" Danni asked, looking around at the women. "I would've thought things got easier."

"Quite the opposite," Summer said with laugh. "Since we began noticing the opposite sex, that's exactly what made things more difficult for us. By sixth grade, most of the girls had a crush on Aiden. That meant with the exception of a few of our close friends, the girls who liked Aiden really disliked me."

"Kind of like how all the boys in sixth grade had a crush on you and would spend basketball and track practice asking me questions about you rather than playing the sport."

Summer's head whipped over her shoulder at the sound of Aiden's deep, melodic voice. She'd seen him a few days ago, but the way he was looking at her made her feel as though it had been much longer.

"Um, how? What?"

Aiden laughed at her incomplete sentences. "Relax, Dupree, I didn't follow you here. My hotel just so happens to be next door and I heard that tonight this lounge was playing live reggae music."

He glanced around at her friends. "Hello, ladies. It's nice to see you all again." They all responded with different versions of hello. Summer would have laughed at the dreamy tones in their voices if she hadn't been so caught off guard by how good Aiden looked in a pair of navy blue pants, crisp white shirt, complementing blue shoes and a navy blue NY Yankees hat. He'd always had style, but while some stuff that Aiden wore would look average on any other man, it was sexy on him.

Girl, you have got to remove the word sexy *from your vocabulary when thinking about Aiden.* It was bad enough she almost checked him out in front of her friends, but now he was staring at her, clearly waiting for her to respond to something he'd asked.

"What did you say?"

He winked at her and smiled. "I asked if it was okay if I joined you ladies."

Danni cleared her throat. "Just for the record, we already told him it was okay if he sat with us."

Of course y'all did. "Yes, that's fine with me. The more the merrier. We have plenty of space. You can sit wherever you want. Any place is fine." *Crap, I sound way too happy. And why in the world am I still talking?*

Not surprisingly, he chose the seat right next to her. His arm brushed against hers as he adjusted himself in his seat. She bit her bottom lip as she glanced at the dance floor. The reggae band took the stage and started playing. Summer had always loved reggae music, so when they sang a Bob Marley jam, she couldn't help but sway in her seat. Soon, she was so wrapped up in the music, she almost forgot that Aiden was sitting right next to her. *Almost*.

"You always did have some great dance moves," he whispered into her ear. She froze in her chair, but continued looking out at the band. "They weren't as good as my moves, though."

"Yeah, right," she whispered back. "You used to wish you had moves like this." She stood from her seat and did a slow hip roll to the beat of the music. She'd never been a shy person, nor did she ignore a challenge.

"You may have been a good dancer back in the day," she said, not bothering to whisper any longer. "But I've always been better."

She finally turned from the dance floor to look at Aiden. When she locked eyes with him, she froze once again.

"You're right, Dupree." He looked her up and down. "Your moves always were better."

She quickly sat back down and tried to ignore the swarm of bees buzzing around in her stomach. This was probably one of those challenges she should have ignored because Aiden Chase didn't play fairly…he didn't play fairly at all.

Chapter 6

For the umpteenth time since she'd arrived at her boutique, Summer wondered how in the world she'd agreed to Aiden's offer to help get the shop ready for the grand opening.

"Stop thinking so hard," Danni said when she walked past Summer. "Since he's going to be including Bare Sophistication in his Miami photo showcase, it seems fitting that he'd help."

After the band had finished playing at the lounge a couple of nights ago, Summer and Aiden had told the women about his idea to feature Bare Sophistication in his exhibit. As expected, they were excited.

"And we need a man around here to lift some of the heavy boxes," Aaliyah added. "It helps that you guys are best friends."

Summer groaned loud enough for all the women to hear. She knew they needed the help, but she would prefer if the man they'd recruited didn't make her lady parts suddenly develop a naughty mind of their own. "We *were* best friends. Now we're just more like two people trying to rebuild a friendship."

"We get the picture," Nicole said with a laugh as she stepped on a stool to wipe the high shelves on the wall. "Why did you guys stop being friends, anyway? No matter what you say, you still seem close."

Without warning, Summer's mind drifted to a bad memory. A time in her life that she tried not to think about. A moment when everything changed in the blink of an eye.

"Um, we just grew apart," she lied. "When we were at the lounge the other day, we just fell into old patterns."

"Well, whataya know," Danni said, walking toward the front door. "Mr. Prince Charming has arrived."

Summer only had a moment to glance at Aiden walking through the door before her iPhone rang. Her condo's management was calling her.

"Hi, Mr. Yale."

"Hi, Summer. I'm sorry to bother you, but we need you to come to the office. There's an issue with your condo."

"What's wrong?" she asked in a worried tone.

"I'd rather explain it in person, but unfortunately, you'll have to be displaced for a little while we fumigate your place."

"Fumigate my place?" Summer glanced at Danni who looked equally as concerned before glancing at Aiden who was studying her intently. She had no doubt he could read the panic on her face. "I'll be right there."

She made it to the management office in twenty minutes. Although she'd told everyone they could stay at the shop, Aaliyah, Nicole and Aiden had accompanied her and were waiting in the lobby of the office. Danni was standing right next to her looking as surprised as Summer felt.

"So, you're saying that I have to leave my condo for five weeks? Mr. Yale, I'm opening a boutique in eight weeks. I can't be displaced for that long."

"I'm so sorry, Summer, but we have to fumigate all three residences in your section of the building. We've never seen an infestation this terrible. Bedbugs, earwigs, centipedes, fleas, ants." Mr. Yale started scratching his arm. "I itch just thinking about what I saw."

"And it all originated from Mr. Higgins apartment?"

"Yes. Apparently, the bugs traveled to your condo and the other one, as well. According to pest control, there are quite a few things living in the walls you share with Mr. Higgins." Now it was Summer's time to scratch her arm.

"Look at that." Mr. Yale pointed to small marks on Summer's and Danni's arms. "You've both probably been getting bit at night and didn't notice."

They both glanced at their arms before looking at each other. Just yesterday morning, they had been discussing a few random bites on their arms and legs.

"Oh, my goodness," Summer said scratching profusely, "I didn't think anything of the bites."

Danni lightly hopped from one foot to the other as she began scratching her neck and arms. "I can't even stand still thinking about it."

"Can we at least pack some of our stuff?" Summer asked.

"Yes, but we have to be really careful. Pest control is still up there and I mentioned that you both would want to gather some things. You only have about thirty minutes. An hour tops. They have already started the first fumigation process. Some of your belongings are already in plastic bags, but you'll have to wash all your clothes before you do anything to avoid infesting wherever you'll be residing for the next five weeks."

Defeated, Summer filled out some paperwork that Mr. Yale needed her approval on and walked out into the lobby to tell the others what had just occurred. They all immediately agreed to help her pack up as much as they could.

When they reached her floor, Summer's anxiety rose as she saw the commotion in the hallway outside of Mr. Higgins's condo. Summer asked the others to head into her place to see what they could do while she spoke to her neighbor. She wasn't surprised that Aiden stayed by her side.

"Mr. Higgins?" Summer called into his apartment trying to get his attention. Her eyes roamed over all the stuff in Mr. Higgins home. Either he was a hoarder or he just happened to have a lot of old junk.

"Wow!" Aiden said from behind her. "No wonder no one knew about the infestation. There's so much junk in here, you can barely see the floor."

"Mr. Higgins," Summer called again when she spotted him. "What is all this stuff?" She waved her hand across his home.

Mr. Higgins shrugged. "My belongings. My nephew collects old furniture that people throw out. Old, worn furniture helps me think when I play my music."

Is this man for real? Just glancing at some of the furniture made her skin crawl. "Listen, Mr. Higgins. I'm not upset about the pest infestation. Things like this happen all the time. What I am upset about is that when you noticed the bugs you didn't say anything to management right away. Preferably before they made a home in our walls."

"They weren't bothering me, so I didn't feel a need to say anything. Besides," he said in an irritated tone. "I don't have to answer to you or anyone else. Whatever I do in my condo is my business. Don't you have anything better to do than harass an old man? Run along, now."

"There's no use talking to you." Summer shrugged off his comment and walked away with Aiden right behind her.

"Is it just me, or does that old man sound like he just walked out of a Shakespearean play?"

"That's exactly what I had thought," Summer said with a laugh. Within twenty minutes, she'd talked to the pest control team, bagged up most of her essentials and gathered all the clothes she could.

"Thank you guys so much," Summer said when they were back outside by Aiden's rental SUV and Nicole's eco-friendly car.

"No problem," Nicole said, before looking between her and Danni. "Where are you guys going to stay for the next five weeks?"

"Well, I'm thinking we can both stay in the loft of the shop. There's a bathroom up there and everything. I was already planning on buying a bed for future boudoir photo shoots."

"How will we get the loft together before the grand opening if we're living up there?" Danni asked.

"You both could stay with me," Nicole suggested.

"I would offer my place," Aaliyah said, "if I wasn't already staying with my sister, her husband and my niece."

"Thanks for the offer, Nicole, but wouldn't we be in the way of your makeup business? And what about your roommate?" Nicole stayed in a huge, luxurious loft with another makeup artist. She definitely had the space for their belongings, but her industrial loft wasn't equipped to handle two more people.

"I can do business anywhere. Clients only come to my home for consultations. One of you could sleep in the bed with me, while the other sleeps on the couch. It's only temporary, so I'm sure Carlos wouldn't mind."

"Or you could always stay with me, Summer."

All four women turned to look at Aiden. "You mean, stay with you in your hotel room?" she asked. "Isn't that weird? If I were going to do that, I could just book a hotel room myself."

Aiden laughed. "Well, I actually just moved into a beach house yesterday, since I'll be in Miami for the next six months."

Summer swallowed her gasp. "You're in Miami for that long?"

"I sure am."

"And you have room at your beach home?"

He smiled. "I sure do. It's actually a town house with two bedrooms. So I can technically accommodate both you and Danni."

"Oh, I can stay with Nicole," Danni said quickly. "But Summer, you should stay with Aiden."

"I agree," Nicole said. "I'm sure having your own room would be way more comfortable than staying on my couch."

"Seems like a great idea to me, too." Aaliyah looked from Aiden to Summer. "My niece already sleeps with me most nights, so I don't even have my own bed or couch space."

Summer slowly looked from each of her friends to

Aiden. She didn't know why, but living with Aiden seemed like a very *very* bad idea.

"Are you sure you want to do this?" She studied his eyes and was sure he noticed the hesitation in hers.

"Absolutely positive." His response was direct and the confidence in his voice could not be denied.

"Okay," she said, completely aware that her voice sounded extremely low. Aiden didn't seem to mind that she was nervous. In fact, he seemed to enjoy her discomfort.

Aiden tried his best not to laugh at the way Summer was squirming in the passenger seat of his car. They'd spent the past five hours at a Laundromat with her friends so that she and Danni could wash all their clothes. At times, he'd catch a glimpse of something of Summer's made of lace or satin, and he'd try his best not to salivate.

They were almost back at the shop so that she could pick up her car and trail him to his beach home. She'd barely spoken two words to him since they'd said their goodbyes to her friends. Although sometimes he liked to see her fidget around, he didn't want her feeling so uncomfortable.

"The boutique is coming along wonderfully," he said, in an effort to break the silence.

"Thanks." She didn't glance at him, but at least she'd responded. "I'm glad you liked the idea of turning the loft into a boudoir studio."

"It's a great idea, and you have the perfect team of women to really promote something like that. The four of you are truly talented. I think the public will react to the boutique really well and I've seen all the media buzz you've got circulating already. Pretty impressive, Dupree."

"Thanks Aiden. It means a lot to hear you say that."

He smiled and continued to focus on the road. When they arrived at her boutique, he decided to address the elephant in the car.

"Summer, I hope you know that I'd never do anything to make you uncomfortable."

She glanced at him before unlocking her door and hopping out of his SUV. "I know you wouldn't. It's just… you and I haven't even been in the same state together for five weeks in a row, let alone the same living space. That's a lot of time together."

He chuckled. "We used to spend every day together."

"Yeah, from, like, age five to fourteen. High school and college were different." At the mention of college, Aiden noticed her face slightly tense. *God, we have so much to talk about.*

"In high school it may have changed to every other day and, yes, we went to different colleges, but we still saw each other on breaks and some weekends."

Her face tensed even more. He really wasn't trying to bring up bad memories before they even got to his temporary home. There weren't many things that Aiden regretted in life, but not being there for Summer at a time when she truly needed him was something he'd never forgive himself for.

"Tell you what. I may have to travel to New York and LA for work, so I'll talk to my business manager and solidify those dates. That way, you'll know what days you'll have the place to yourself."

He noticed that she finally began to relax. "That's not necessary," she said with a laugh. "I'm just overreacting when I should be thanking you for opening up your home to me. We've known each other for years, so I'm sure it won't be that difficult living together for the next few weeks."

"Exactly. It'll be fine. We've been meaning to catch up for years, so what better way for two friends to catch up than sharing the same living space for a while?"

"That's very true. We do have a lot to catch up on."

"So, does that mean you won't regret your decision to stay with me?"

She squinted her eyes as she studied his face. He tried not to glance at her perfectly shaped lips, but he couldn't help it. Her mouth parted slightly when she caught his blatant stare.

"Just remember, I know you better than most, Aiden." She leaned a little closer in the cab of the car. "Working on our friendship means things stay platonic between us, right? Because based on that look in your eyes, it seems like you're up to no good."

Up to no good, indeed. No, he didn't want things to stay platonic. Yes, he wanted to work on their friendship. No, his thoughts weren't as innocent as they should be. Nonetheless, he wanted Summer to trust him.

"Trust me, Summer. We've already missed out on years of being in each other's lives. While you stay with me, we'll just be two friends catching up on old times."

She nodded her head in agreement and seemed to believe him. Now all he had to do was believe himself.

Chapter 7

"**Y**ou're an idiot," he said aloud to himself as he jogged along the beach. Unlike usual, he wasn't even listening to music as he jogged. The thoughts in his mind were ricocheting all over the place, creating enough annoying sounds to last a lifetime.

It was Tuesday night and Summer had been living with him for eight days, fourteen hours, and twenty-two minutes. In that time, Aiden had taken more cold showers than he ever thought possible. On day three, Summer had commented that she never knew he enjoyed taking so many showers. He'd made up some story about showers contributing to a photographer's success. Little did she know, he took two showers a day only so that he wouldn't embarrass himself by being hard in front of her all the time.

On day four—the one day he thought he'd finally gotten his male urges under control—she came walking through the door wearing some tight pink spandex leggings and a black tank top, having just come from a

Pilates class with her friends. Aiden took an hour-long cold shower that day.

On day five she'd gone out with the girls to some natural hair event, so she'd pulled her curls into a pineapple style on top of her head and worn a deep purple lace dress that had pissed him off the minute he saw her wearing it. He wasn't the type of man who cared if the woman he was interested in looked good going out. In fact, he was definitely more the type that would look at other men and say, "Yeah, she belongs to me. See it and weep."

Yet on this particular night—when his desire for her had reached an entirely new level—she had come walking out of her bedroom wearing a dress made of all lace and all he could imagine was her in lace panties, instead. No bra.

She'd looked good. Even better than good. She'd been mouthwatering. He'd barely been able to keep his eyes off her as she walked out of the house. When Dax had called to ask him if he could fly to LA the next morning, Aiden had happily agreed. His body needed a break from Summer.

Aiden didn't date a lot, but when he used his charm on a woman he found attractive, it seemed natural that she'd end up in his bed before the night was over. Traveling all over the world meant women knew he couldn't commit to them. Yet living with Summer was proving to be much more difficult than he'd originally thought. They hadn't really hung out, since she'd been busy at the shop and he'd been taking photos for his exhibit. And when he did help her at the shop, her friends were usually there, too.

He'd just arrived back in Miami a few hours ago and, luckily, Summer had been at the boutique.

"What the hell was I thinking making that promise?" He'd never experienced this much angst over a woman he'd promised not to touch…embrace…kiss. As a matter of fact, he'd never even wanted a woman as much as he wanted Summer. It almost felt like he was in some strange twenty-year twilight zone. Fighting off the attraction was finally coming to a head. Literally and figuratively.

As the sun set, he made his way back to his town house noting that Summer's car wasn't parked in its normal spot. *Great. She's still not home yet.* He shouldn't have been so happy about that fact, but he was. He needed to regain his composure before seeing her.

The moment he opened the back door, he could hear the light humming of Summer's sweet voice traveling through the house. *So, she is home.* He'd almost forgotten how gifted she was vocally. She'd always been able to sing better than anyone in middle and high school. He followed the sound of her voice and spotted her in the hallway lying on her back and looking through the skylight window.

Her flowy white shirt had fallen off one shoulder and she was wearing a pair of green cotton shorts that accentuated her amazingly beautiful calves and legs. It wasn't just her simple, yet cute, outfit that caught Aiden's attention. It was the way she was lying on the hallway floor. Her butt was almost pushed all the way to the wall with her legs at a seventy-five degree angle. For runners, it was a great way to stretch the lower body. However, Aiden had known Summer too long to know that she didn't just lie in that position when she wanted to stretch. For whatever reason, she always lay that way when she was thinking hard about something.

She stretched an arm across her face and tapped her feet on the wall as she continued to sing. He knew he should make his presence known, but he wasn't quite done observing her yet. *Hmm, I wonder what she's thinking about.* He ignored the part of his consciousness that hoped she was thinking about him just as much as he'd been thinking about her.

Fifteen years ago...

Aiden counted to ten in his head before he opened the door to the walk-in closet. His heart was beating extremely fast, and he didn't think he could slow it down even if he tried.

The lights were off, but one of those circular battery operated lights sat in the corner of the closet. That's where he found Summer.

"What are you doing? Stretching your legs?" he asked as he sat beside her. She was lying on the floor with her butt pressed against the wall and her legs in the air.

"No. When I lie like this, I do some of my best thinking."

"Okay," he said with a laugh. "And what could you possibly be thinking about in a closet?"

She dropped her legs to the side and leaned up to sit beside him. "I was thinking about how odd it is that out of almost sixteen sophomore boys at this party, I pulled your name out of a hat."

Aiden nodded his head in understanding. He'd wondered the same thing. "We don't have to do anything, Summer. It isn't some rite of passage that says at we have to actually play seven minutes of heaven. We can just pretend to participate in the kissing game."

He didn't want to tell her that he was actually glad she'd chosen his name. It wasn't that he expected a kiss or anything. After all, they were best friends and kissing your best friend could be weird. He was just glad whenever he got to spend time with her alone.

"Yeah, we can pretend. And you can tell Rochelle that nothing happened."

"Rochelle isn't my girlfriend. I told you that." He'd been dealing with Rochelle's crush on him since middle school.

"I know what you said, but I also know that she still likes you."

"Well, Sam still likes you, too. Does that mean you won't kiss me because of Sam?" Summer's eyes grew wide and he immediately realized his mistake. "What I meant is, if hypothetically we did kiss, should I feel bad because Sam likes you? Justin likes you, too. Should I feel bad about him?"

"I guess not," she said after a few seconds of silence. "I mean, hypothetically it wouldn't matter."

A minute passed without either of them saying anything. He had no idea how long they'd been in the closet or how much time they had left.

"So, what if we did kiss?" Summer asked as she fidgeted with the edge of her shirt. "Would it be weird, since we're best friends?"

He studied her face as he contemplated his response. "I don't think it would be weird. Do you?"

She looked in his eyes before dropping her gaze to his lips. *You know you want to kiss her*, the voice inside his head taunted. It wasn't the first time he'd heard that voice and he doubted it would be the last. He'd never tell Summer how much he wanted to kiss her, but judging by the way she was looking at him, he had a feeling she wanted to kiss him just as badly.

"No, I don't think it would be weird."

His heart started beating even faster than it had when he'd walked into the closet. "We probably have three or four minutes left. Do you want to kiss and just get it over with?"

She nodded her head. "Yes, I say we try it. We've both kissed people before. What's the worst that could happen?"

"Right, what's the worst that could happen?" he agreed, as he started leaning in toward Summer. She began leaning toward him, too, and soon they were so close he could feel her breath teasing his lips.

"You sure?" He lightly touched her chin with his hand.

"Yes," she whispered.

His lips touched hers gently, with just enough pressure. They hadn't discussed if it would be a closed-lips kiss or a lips-and-tongue kiss, so Aiden wasn't sure what he should do next. Up until this point, he'd really only had PG-13 kisses with other girls, and knowing Summer, she'd had the same experience with the boys she'd kissed. Already, this kiss with Summer wasn't feeling like anything he'd ever experienced.

Mustering up everything he'd ever thought about doing if he got a chance to kiss Summer, he let his tongue brush against her lips. At her gasp, he slipped his tongue inside her mouth, encouraged by her appreciative moan. She was getting into the kiss just as much as he was, and before he knew what was happening, her tongue was stroking his right back.

What in the world are we doing and why have we never done this before? Aiden felt the kiss in every part of his body, and Summer was clinging to his shirt and making sounds that he'd never heard before when making out with a girl. He could definitely tell that their kiss was exploratory, but they'd found a good rhythm pretty fast.

At the sound of the knock on the door, they jumped away from each other. Their seven minutes were up and it was time for another couple to enter the closet. Aiden stood and helped Summer stand up, as well. They always got teased about secretly liking each other and Aiden knew it would only be worse now. Summer was flushed and blushing like crazy. He knew he probably looked just as disconcerted. There was no way they could hide it from all their classmates on the other side of the door.

"See, nothing bad happened," Summer said with an uncertain smile. Aiden didn't say anything. He couldn't say anything. She may have convinced herself that nothing bad had happened, but in his mind, the worst *possible* thing had happened. He'd kissed his best friend and he'd liked it. A lot. Even worse, Summer wanted him to act like nothing had changed. *Yeah, right.*

He knew better. After a kiss like that, things were bound to be different. At this age, his body was already changing and he was feeling emotions that he'd never felt before. Summer may be able to brush off the kiss, but Aiden was sure the kiss they'd just shared would be branded in his mind forever.

Present day...

"Um, Aiden? Is everything okay?"

He could hear Summer's voice, but he was still lost in thought. "I'm sorry, what did you say?"

She rolled to the side and stood up from the floor.

"You were just standing there staring at me with a dorky smile on your face," she laughed. "So I asked if everything was…" Her voice trailed off as something else took her interest. He followed her gaze and looked down at his jogging pants.

"Oh, shit." He grabbed a book off his mahogany hallway table and put it in front of his pants. "Sorry. I was just lost in thought. I should have announced that I was home since you had on your headphones. I didn't mean to startle you."

She looked from his face, back down to the book, then up to his face again. "What were you thinking about?"

"Come again?"

"You said you were lost in thought. What were you thinking about?"

Baby, you definitely do NOT want to know. "Um, I was thinking about this really nice photo I took at the airport when my plane landed earlier today."

She looked unconvinced. "So, thinking about an airport photo made you…" She glanced at the book again. "Excited?"

"Yeah, didn't you hear?" he said with a forced laugh. "Planes are the new porn. I just can't get enough of looking at them."

"Well, that's funny, because I thought maybe seeing me lying against the wall like that made you think about the first time we kissed in that closet for seven minutes of heaven." She smiled as she stepped closer to him. "So it's good to know that you don't get hard when thinking about me, but rather about big planes. Who knew?"

He raised an eyebrow at her. "Your sarcasm is not appreciated right now."

"I thought it was pretty funny," she said with a shrug.

"Anyway, I'm glad you're here because I was just about to watch *The Godfather*. Care to join me?"

The Godfather was one of his favorite movies and he didn't doubt that it would break the sexual tension. "Yeah, I'm down for watching a movie." He glanced down at the book. "I just need to take a cold shower first."

"Take all the time you need, lover boy," she said with a smile as she patted him on the shoulder.

"You can't touch me right now."

She laughed as she moved her hand away. He hadn't been called "lover boy" since high school. He still didn't care for the nickname, but it was nice to know that they could joke about their attraction without it being too awkward.

Chapter 8

This is so awkward, Summer thought as she adjusted herself on the couch for the fourth time in thirty seconds. It was hard enough ignoring her attraction to him without the added third party in the room, who'd decided to pay them a visit an hour ago.

Even though she'd asked Aiden if he wanted to watch a movie with her, she didn't think he'd sit so close to her on the couch. Close enough for her to pick up on how amazing he smelled after a shower. Close enough that she couldn't ignore how sexy he looked in basketball shorts and a white T-shirt. *Oh, man, my body hasn't been this in tune with a man in...well, ever!* Who told him it was okay to cause her discomfort in an area that would remain nameless? It had been difficult enough trying to silence her attraction when they were in high school, but now again, as an adult? Not. Fair. At. All.

"Do you want to watch *Titanic* instead?" he asked, breaking into her thoughts.

"Now?"

He looked from the movie to her. "Yeah, since neither

one of us seems to be into this movie at the moment. *Titanic* was another one we liked."

"You hardly liked it," she said with a laugh. "You can only watch the movie if we act out the good scenes. I actually like the entire movie."

"That's not true. I also like it for the special effects."

"Okay, so you like it for the special effects and the fact that we act out the scenes."

"Exactly." He looked back to the movie, but she doubted he was actually watching it. "So, are we changing the movie?"

Summer adjusted herself yet again so that she wasn't so close to him. "Aren't we a little too old to be acting out *Titanic*?"

He clamped his hand over his heart as if he was offended. "No, you didn't just diss Leonardo and Kate's love."

She slightly threw back her head in a laugh. "You mean Jack and Rose?"

He gave her a blank stare. "No one remembers their names in the movie. They will always be Leonardo and Kate. If it were up to me, they'd be married today."

Summer laughed even harder, and eventually Aiden broke out in a wide grin. Without waiting for her okay, he took *The Godfather* out of the DVD player and put in *Titanic*.

"Prepare to lose, Dupree. My acting skills were already better than yours." He stretched and began running in place as if he were preparing for a boxing match instead of some movie reenactments.

"I didn't know we were competing over who's the better actor," she said in between laughs.

He gave her a look of disbelief. "We're always competing, but I assume you only said that because you were always the worst when it came to reenacting scenes."

Ten minutes into the movie, she was still laughing at Aiden's crazy antics. Twenty minutes into the movie, she realized he was right. He was a much better actor than she was. There were so many things she'd missed about him, but the way he made her laugh just by being himself was by far the thing she missed the most.

As it neared the first scene where Jack and Rose meet as Jack tries to save her from jumping off the back of the ship, it took all of Summer's energy to control her laughter.

"Are you going to keep laughing?"

"I'm sorry." She fanned herself. "Okay, I'm ready. But you can't expect me not to laugh when you get so engrossed in playing Leonardo."

She walked over to the chair in the corner of the room, to use it as a platform to lean against so she could pretend it was the edge of the ship.

She rolled her neck and did a little hop, mimicking Aiden when he was preparing to act out a scene. "Okay, let's do this." She leaned against the chair as she glanced behind her to view the scene on the television.

"I changed my mind," he said from behind her. "How about I pretend to be myself, instead."

When did he get so close? His breath fanned the side of her neck. "Don't come any closer," she said mimicking the scene. "I mean it. I'll let go."

"No, you won't," he whispered in her ear. "I know you, Summer. You can't let go and neither can I."

She sucked in a deep breath at his nearness. "Those are the lines."

"I know." He moved to whisper in her other ear. "I'm

done acting. Done pretending. At least for tonight. You were right. We're too old to play games."

As Summer kept her eyes trained on the television, she was extremely aware of the seductive tone in Aiden's voice. A tone that didn't embody any of the comical innuendos he'd been using earlier.

She was sure that now was the time for her to respond, but her words were so jumbled in her mind, she wasn't sure she could even formulate a complete sentence out loud. Instead, she leaned against his body as opposed to the chair.

As he always did, he wrapped his arms around her and placed his head in the curve of her neck. When they were younger, she'd never understood why some of her friends would claim that she and Aiden didn't hug in a friend's sort of way, but rather a lover's sort of way. At the time, she didn't understand what they meant. Of course she'd realized their hugs had progressed after the kiss they'd shared in the closet. However, she still hadn't really understood what they meant. Until now...

Her backside pressed against his front, his arms wrapped around her and his forehead against her skin felt intimate. Private. It felt like a hug between two people who were in tune with each other. Summer wasn't even sure if she could keep saying they were just friends anymore. Nothing felt the same, yet everything felt the same. It was so confusing.

Of its own accord, her body molded more into his and she leaned her head back to give him better access to her neck. The light groan that escaped his lips sent tingles throughout her entire body, and within seconds she felt his lips lightly brush the exposed area. In an effort to control her moans as he placed sweet, tender kisses all across her skin, she rolled her head to the side. The movement only made him switch from kissing one side of her neck to the other. The touch of his lips on her skin felt so good, she couldn't help but squirm a little. Then he placed his hands on either side of her thighs to keep her in place.

You should do something. She just wasn't sure what that something was. Should she lean more into him? Turn around to face him? Maybe she should move out of his embrace to the other side of the room.

His hands began massaging her thighs, which made her shorts tighten, causing the most delicious friction against her core. *Okay, so moving out of his embrace is definitely not an option.* She wasn't even sure her feet could move at the moment anyway. She was vaguely aware that her inner thighs were producing more heat than bacon crackling on a hot pan.

With his hands and lips on her at the same time, she couldn't think straight. All she could do was feel. She leaned her head back even more and glanced up to look at him. *Oh, my.* The thoughts reflected in his eyes weren't guarded, but instead left open for her to analyze. He'd promised he wouldn't do anything that wasn't considered friendly, so she assumed that also meant kissing. *But you want to kiss him.* Oh, she wanted to kiss him badly. When he reached out a hand and ran it through her hair, a little more of her resilience broke.

What's one tiny kiss? she thought as she took control of the situation, turned around to face him, and leaned on tiptoes to place a soft kiss on his lips. At least, soft had been the idea until her lips actually crashed onto his. Instead of soft and slow, the kiss was all-consuming and demanded every part of her to pay attention. When she'd first kissed Aiden when they were fifteen years old, she hadn't really known what she was doing. She'd thought that maybe she'd French-kissed a boy before Aiden, but the moment his tongue had played with hers in that closet, she'd realized she had never *ever* been kissed like that before.

They'd shared a few kisses after that, but this kiss right now felt slightly different. They weren't two kids learning how the other tasted for the first time. Now they were adults and much more experienced in the art form.

His tongue slipped into her mouth at the same time his arms pulled her closer and his expert lips moved exquisitely across hers. She wasn't even sure she'd remember her own name if someone asked her.

Her hands moved underneath his shirt and she ran her fingers across his pectoral muscles. Eventually her hands made their way to the back of his head as she slipped her tongue even deeper. The groan he released was so strong, she shivered at the fact that she had gotten him so worked up with one kiss.

His hands moved to her lower back and soon she felt the cool surface of the wall. Her thighs lifted of their own accord and as she'd hoped, Aiden grasped her to hold her in place. Within seconds, they were grinding fully clothed against the barrier and kissing so passionately that she wasn't sure who was leading the kiss anymore.

Him. Definitely him... Only Aiden could kiss her so thoroughly. So completely. He held her effortlessly and as seconds turned to minutes, everything around her blurred.

"Damn, I've wanted to kiss you since I saw you outside your boutique," he said into her mouth.

She'd wanted to kiss him, too, but for *so* much longer. *If your life hadn't spiraled out of control in college, you could have had him.* That timid voice in the back of her mind crept to the surface, reminding her once again of what she'd lost. Time that she'd never be able to get back. Reasons she and Aiden could never be the Summer and Aiden she'd imagined.

Mustering all the strength she could, she broke off the kiss, but Aiden didn't let her feet touch the ground. He only looked confused for a few seconds before his expression changed to acknowledgment.

Don't get emotional. Don't get emotional. She chanted the words over and over in her mind, determined to keep her face as expressionless as possible.

Aiden leaned his forehead against hers. "We have to talk about it, Summer."

"There's nothing to discuss," she said quickly.

He lifted his head, peering at her as he released her thighs from his hands. Her body immediately missed his touch.

"Do you really believe that?" he asked. "You think there's nothing for us to discuss?"

"I do." She shrugged and shuffled from one foot to the other. Her heart rate had finally started to slow down. "I didn't mean to kiss you, so just forget it happened."

"Don't ever apologize for kissing me." Aiden leaned closer to her, and to her surprise, she stood in place and didn't falter. "We don't have to talk right now, but eventually we will. After all these years, you have to understand why I want to talk about it."

She averted her eyes before looking back at him. "Can we just finish acting out the movie?"

A sly smile crept across his face. "Of course we can." He plopped back down on the couch and grabbed the remote. "How about I fast-forward to the part where Jack and Kate dance?"

"Why?" she asked, joining him on the couch.

"Well, if I fast-forward to that scene, then you'll have to do some dancing." He grinned. "Or maybe I'll fast-forward to the scene where Jack paints Kate in the nude. Think you're up for it?"

She knew he was joking, but she still got butterflies in her stomach. "You can't be serious."

"Says who? When do I ever joke about seeing you naked? Do you remember when I dared you to skinny-dip if you lost that card game?"

"How could I forget?" she asked with a laugh. "After I lost, you wouldn't drop it and teased me the entire night."

"You damn right I teased you," he said, laughing along with her. "You never turned down a dare, but you thought it would be okay to turn down that one?"

"Of course I did. It involved me being naked. I didn't want our entire class to see me naked. I didn't even want you to see me naked." *Not entirely true, but oh, well!*

"Oh, that's right." He snapped his fingers in recognition. "I forgot you had that third nipple that you were always worried about me seeing."

"I did not and do not have a third nipple," she said, punching him in the arm.

"Oh, then you must be talking about that brown birthmark on your butt that's shaped like a perfect heart."

She froze. "You saw my birthmark?" It was smack-dab in the middle of her right cheek, so there weren't too many people who knew that it was there.

He stopped laughing as his eyes dropped to her lips again. "I saw everything that night."

His penetrating stare seemed to pierce right through her.

Summer sat up a little straighter on the couch as his stare intensified, his eyes never faltering from hers. She gave her mind a mental shake for forgetting how easily Aiden could go from annoying, to charming, to downright seductive. The man had been born with a gift and he wasn't ashamed to use it. She knew from experience that once Aiden Chase put his mind to something, he was all hands in. Literally.

Twelve years ago...

"Aiden, come on. This was a stupid dare. I'll do anything else." Summer glanced at all their friends standing along the edge of the water waiting for her to skinny-dip.

"No can do, Dupree. A bet's a bet and you lost."

Summer groaned as she looked at Aiden. She knew that look. He wasn't going to let her out easily. Sometimes, she forgot how competitive he was.

"Don't you remember when you made me streak in the gym last year?"

Oh, right, I did make him do that. Whoops! "No, I have no idea what you're talking about."

"Oh, really?" Aiden said with a laugh. "I think the exact words that you and the other girls in our class chanted were 'Aiden, man up and do the dare. You know you lost fair and square. So lose those clothes and lose them quick, because you just lost to a chick.' And a lot of the girls changed the last part to rhyme with something else, but I'm not even gonna go there."

"I can't believe you're making me do this." She had never backed down from a dare, but skinny-dipping in front of half the class wasn't remotely close to what she wanted to be doing after senior prom. She was looking forward to relaxing at the lake house they'd all chipped in to rent, not show everyone how she looked naked. Although she was looking forward to leaving Claysville, she still wanted to have one last celebration with her classmates.

"What's taking so long, Dupree?"

She cut her eyes at Aiden and mouthed the words *I hate you.* "Just remember that I plan to pay you back," she said wading up to her knees into the water. At least it was dark outside, so people wouldn't really see her. She wasn't stupid. There was no way she was leaving her clothes on the ground. She was bringing everything in with her and would strip under the water. She was pretty sure that was what Aiden wanted her to do, anyway.

Of course that's what he wants me to do. An idea sparked. She doubted Aiden wanted her taking off her clothes in front of any of the guys, so she decided to tease him. She waded back to shore and began lifting her shirt as if she were taking it off. As predicted, Aiden jumped in front of her when it was only a couple of inches high.

"What are you doing, Aiden?" one of the guys yelled.

Aiden ignored him and turned his head to her. "Summer, what are you doing? Why aren't you going under in the water to block yourself?"

"What's the matter, Aiden?" she whispered. "You made the dare. Don't want any of the boys to see me naked?"

"Not a chance," he whispered back. "I'm the only one who should see you naked."

His head jerked back to hers so fast, she knew he realized his mistake. "I mean…well, I don't want the guys… wait, that's not how I meant it."

He's stuttering. She smiled at him. Aiden only stuttered when he'd accidentally said something he'd rather keep to himself.

"Forget this," another guy yelled to all their classmates. "It's our last time being together and we'll probably never see one another again. Let's all skinny-dip!" Within minutes, clothes were flying everywhere as people ran into the water. Some nude. Some still wearing their underwear. Others were fully clothed. To Summer's surprise, it seemed to be less about the nudity and more about enjoying one last hurrah.

"What do you say?" Summer asked Aiden. "Since we're both going to schools in California, we'll only be a few hours apart. But who knows how much we'll see each other?"

Aiden glanced around the lake and Summer followed his gaze that had landed on a tree that was partially in the water and partially on land.

"I'll race you to that spot," Aiden said, removing his shirt and taking off running. Summer followed his lead, removing her top layered shirt as she caught up with him. When they reached the tree, she noticed it formed a cove that was semiprivate. In the dark, she assumed others couldn't see much, despite the lights along the lake.

"You getting in or what?" Aiden asked as he began unbuttoning his jeans. Summer hesitated, surprised he was actually undressing.

"What are you doing?"

"Skinny-dipping," he said, slipping off his jeans completely and kicking his gym shoes to the side at the same time. She'd already removed her top shirt, but she hadn't removed her tank or anything else. *Well, I guess he's seen me in a bikini, so wearing my bra and panties isn't a big deal.* She slid off her tank and flip-flops before she unbuttoned and removed her wet jeans. By the time she'd finished, she saw Aiden in her peripheral vision, removing what looked to be his boxers.

She glanced over at him and froze. *Holy Mother Nature.* All thoughts washed from her mind as she stood there glancing at Aiden in all his naked glory. *Shy he is not,* she thought as he walked toward her wearing a confident smile.

"You can leave on your underwear if you want, Dupree." He waded into the water and leaned against the tree. "But you only live once."

She knew what he was doing. He was baiting her. And it was working. "I'm not getting my hair wet," she said as she turned her back to him and unclasped her bra. She tossed it on top of her jeans, then removed her panties and tossed them aside, too. She glanced over her shoulder at Aiden after she was completely nude. The passionate look on his face made her breath catch. She wasn't sure what happened in that moment, but a wave of confidence washed over her as she finally turned to join him in the water.

He lifted a wet hand and ran it down her arm. She shivered beneath his touch and leaned closer to him. "What about our prom dates?" she asked as she placed her head in the crook of his neck. His hands began roaming all over her body and the pleasure his touch evoked was so strong, she could hardly stand.

"I'm not thinking about our prom dates," Aiden said. "I wanted to ask you to prom, but you'd already said yes to someone else."

Summer lifted her head from his shoulder. "You wanted to ask me to prom?"

"Of course I did." He began rubbing his thumb in

circles along her spine. "Who else would I rather take to prom than you?"

Summer let out a disappointed sigh. "I'd wanted to go with you, too, but I assumed you didn't want to make things awkward."

"Things with you are never awkward," Aiden said as he began kissing her neck. His hands moved from her lower back to the apex of her thighs. Of their own accord, her thighs opened, giving him better access to the part that really craved his attention.

With each kiss he placed on her body, his hands grew bolder until, finally, he slipped a finger inside her core.

"Aiden." She whispered his name as his fingers moved inside her. They hadn't kissed since they'd played seven minutes of heaven and they definitely hadn't done anything like what they were doing now.

Summer dipped one hand beneath the water and began rubbing his length in long, languid strokes.

"Damn, Summer," he muttered as he adjusted the motion of his hand to match the rhythm of hers. His voice was so coarse, Summer barely recognized it.

Her knees began to buckle and her legs began to shake the more he moved his fingers inside her. Before she could comprehend what was going on, she moaned into the night as a rush of desire floated through her body. Despite the onslaught of pleasure, she managed to keep her hand moving along Aiden's length. Within seconds, he threw back his head in a groan and joined her in his own release.

After they both started to come out of their erotic fog, Aiden didn't loosen the grip of his arm around her waist. He stared at her with concern. "Are you okay?"

She smiled. "I'm perfect." He returned her smile before he dipped his head and captured her lips. Her hands immediately went around his neck. Suddenly, it didn't matter that they were friends. It didn't matter that they'd gone to prom with other people. It didn't matter they were going to different colleges. All that mattered was cherishing the moment and enjoying just how right his lips felt on hers.

Chapter 9

"Oh, Winter, that's awesome! I'm so excited for you and Taheim."

"Thanks, sis," Winter replied on the other line. "We still have six months to go. We wanted to tell everyone the minute we found out, but we decided to wait until after the first trimester. We just told Autumn and Ajay right before I called you. They are already sending text messages about everything they want to do with him or her."

Summer smiled as she listened to Winter explain Taheim's initial reaction when she told him she was pregnant. Being a clothing designer, Taheim had already started working on a gender-neutral wardrobe until they found out the sex of the baby. Summer could hear her brother-in-law in the background talking about all the clothes he still wanted to design.

"I can't wait to meet my niece or nephew. You're going to be an amazing mom, sis."

Winter grew quiet on the other line and Summer was

sure she was thinking about what a terrible mother they'd had growing up.

"You won't be anything like her," Summer added, just in case Winter had any doubts.

"Thanks, sis. I know I won't. Taheim and I also decided we're going to visit Dad in France this Thanksgiving. Autumn said she's spending Thanksgiving with the Reeds, so you're more than welcome to spend Thanksgiving with the Reeds, too."

Autumn was engaged to Taheim's brother, Ajay. Every time Summer thought about her sisters and the fact that they'd ended up with brothers, all she could do was smile. They were always so close growing up that it just made sense they'd marry into the same family.

"Oh, and before I forget, Malik mentioned that you never RSVP'd for the joint Thanksgiving-Christmas celebration at his cabin in Michigan next week."

"I know. I meant to tell him that I may not make it. I'm still trying to get the shop together."

"Well, everyone needs a break and we would love to see you. Malik rented two of his neighbors' cabins, as well, so there is plenty of room. Since we'll all be in different places over the holidays, he figured he'd have a pre-holiday celebration."

Their cousins Malik and Micah Madden also lived in Chicago. Malik and his wife, Mya, had a home in Chicago and a cabin in Michigan that they often stayed at throughout the year. Summer was still surprised that both her sisters and two of her six male cousins ended up in Chicago, but since Winter, Autumn, Malik and Micah had all married Chicagoans, it made perfect sense that they lived there now.

While Summer and her sisters had grown up in New

Jersey, her cousins had been raised in Arkansas by their aunt Cynthia and her uncle Mason. Cynthia Madden was nothing like her sister Sonia, and luckily, Summer and her sisters were able to visit or talk to their aunt whenever they needed some womanly advice.

"Okay, I'll try my best to make it."

"Great, and if Danni or Aiden don't have any plans, you can bring them, too."

Summer laughed. "You're not subtle at all. I'm sure you planned on telling Danni yourself, so if you want me to invite Aiden, all you have to do is say so."

"Fine. Summer, can you please invite Aiden? Autumn and I really miss him and we'd love to catch up. And Danni already knows and she wants to come."

"Okay, I'll invite him and talk to Danni."

"Thanks! Guess I'll talk to you soon. Love you!"

"Love you, too."

Summer disconnected the call and glanced out of her window at the sun rising over the ocean. Even though her living quarters were only temporary, she didn't think she'd every tire of seeing the sun rise or set from the view they had in almost every window of the town house.

When she'd awaken an hour ago, she could hear Aiden moving around in the house. It had been three days since they'd shared an intense kiss, which meant her lady parts were *screaming* for a release. She knew living together would be difficult, but spending eleven days under the same roof with a man as tempting as Aiden was way harder than she'd ever imagined.

Since he'd been busy taking photos for his exhibit and she'd been busy at Bare Sophistication, they hadn't seen much of each other. Summer knew that life really was hectic right now for the both of them, but she also knew that they were good at avoiding each other when needed. Just yesterday, she'd been doing yoga in the living room, since she thought he'd mentioned that he would be home late. She hadn't known when he arrived home, but she'd heard his appreciative whistle right in the middle of one of her poses, which had caused her to lose her balance. He raced to her side and attempted to catch her, but they'd ended up in a tangle of limbs on the floor, which, of course, turned into a much more intimate moment. When they actually did communicate, she could really tell they were rebuilding their friendship.

So what if the sexual tension is so thick you can slice it with a knife? The important thing to remember was that they keep the lines of communication open. They were both taking the day off and that meant she couldn't stay cooped up in her room all day.

She glanced down at her tank top and shorts. She should really change out of her pajamas and put on some workout clothes. It was the perfect morning for a beach run. *I wonder if Aiden would want to join me.* They used to run together all the time.

She cracked open her bedroom door to see if she could still hear movement in the house. When all she heard was silence, she tiptoed to the kitchen to see if he was there. Just as she had been staring out her bedroom window, he was looking out the kitchen window holding a mug that she assumed was filled with cinnamon tea, since he'd loved drinking that for as long as she could remember.

With his back turned toward her, she had the chance to admire his physique without him knowing. Even in a plain gray T-shirt, his upper body was impressive, with well-defined biceps and contoured back muscles that she'd only gotten a peek at when she occasionally caught him walking from the bathroom to his bedroom after a shower. Since she'd been staying with him, he'd probably caught her admiring his upper body at least once a day.

As droolworthy as it was, his backside often made her mouth dry. Aiden had never liked his butt, and Summer had always assumed it was because so many girls had always talked about it. What he didn't understand was that she'd never seen a butt so squeezable in her life. Add muscular thighs to that equation and her thoughts went from playful to downright naughty.

His skin always looked so smooth and his complexion flawless. If you didn't know some of the things Aiden had gone through, you'd swear he'd never had a rough day in his life. She thought back to her observation about his complexion. *Definitely hazelnut dipped in a rich chocolate-caramel blend.* Back in the day, she hadn't been the only one well aware of how attractive he was. It seemed almost every girl in school had shamelessly flirted with Aiden. They hadn't called him "lover boy" in high school because he dated a lot of girls. Quite the opposite, in fact. Aiden preferred to only have one steady girlfriend at a time.

He'd gotten the nickname because Aiden was the epitome of every girl's fantasy. He was charming. Athletic. Good-looking. And genuinely a nice guy. He had the persona of the boy next door with the dangerously sexy looks of a bad boy your parents would warn you to stay away from. It almost seemed unfair that he was so blessed.

"How long are you going to stand there and watch me?"

She gasped. *Busted!* He looked over his shoulder and caught her gaze.

"I was just making sure everything was okay," she

lied. He squinted his eyes in observation before turning back to the window.

"No, you weren't."

"Okay," she said, coming from around the edge of the wall. "I actually wanted to know if you wanted to take a run with me."

His eyes perused her attire, shooting a blast of heat through her body. "I think that's a great idea. It's such a beautiful day that I was thinking we could take a canoe ride in Crandon Park. I have a couple shots I want to take."

"Sure, I've never been there. So, you aren't taking the day off?"

"I'm not taking shots for my exhibit. I want to take a few nature shots."

"Sounds good. I'll go put on my running clothes." She was almost to the hallway before she forgot Winter's request.

"Also, I spoke to Winter and she reminded me that my cousin Malik is planning a last-minute pre-holiday party at his Michigan cabin. I'm leaning toward going, so if you can make it, my family would love to see you."

"I'm sure I can make it. I miss them, too."

"Great!"

When she was back in her room, she quickly discarded her pajamas in exchange for some black and baby blue workout capris and a baby blue tank. She threw on her favorite running shoes and grabbed a light black jacket. Once she reached her door, a light sparkle caught her eye. *My locket...* She grabbed the piece of jewelry from her necklace stand and clasped it around her neck. Lately, she hadn't been wearing it whenever she was around Aiden and she wasn't exactly sure why she'd made that decision.

Probably because now that you're around the real him, you don't need the locket. She dismissed the thought as soon as it popped into her mind. The locket had brought her plenty of comfort throughout the years. But now that Aiden was back in her life at the moment, everything felt better than it had in a very long time.

There was something so nostalgic about taking photos of beautiful Crandon Park with Summer. For once, he wasn't imagining that she was with him, walking by his side. She was actually here. They were finally in the same place at the same time. He felt like he'd waited years to have a moment like this.

"It's really peaceful here," she said, as they walked past a beautiful lake and a fountain. There weren't a lot of tourists and it was pretty silent that early in the morning.

"It is. I've been here quite a few times since I moved here." He watched her walk to the edge of the lake and close her eyes as she breathed in the fresh air. He expected her to open her eyes, but after about ten seconds, they remained closed. Aiden lifted his camera to view her through the lens.

She was so beautiful. Always had been. And it wasn't just her outer beauty that had often left him speechless. It was her inner beauty, too. She'd always been one of the most confident girls he knew, and because her life at home was so difficult, she loved school.

Summer always teased him about the girls liking him, but all the boys in school had liked her just as much. He couldn't count how many times he'd had to listen to a guy talk about wanting to take Summer on a date or ask her to a dance. Occasionally, one of those guys would be a friend and they would ask him if he'd mind if they asked her out. *Every* time he had to pretend that he didn't care. Deep down, he didn't want her going out with any guy if it wasn't him.

That was the hard thing about falling for your best friend. On one hand, you already have this amazing friendship to build a relationship on. Yet, on the other hand, if you enter a relationship with each other and it doesn't work, you may have ruined the best connection you ever had with someone.

Summer had always been afraid that they would venture into uncharted waters and ruin their relationship. Seeing that they hadn't really talked in years, Aiden wondered if she still felt the same way.

He watched the rise and fall of her chest as she tilted her head upward to let the sun beam on her face. After their run, she'd let down her ponytail and her hair became a curly mass blowing in the wind. Aiden couldn't remember the last time he saw her look so content.

Kneeling, he found the perfect angle through his lens. The sunlight was hitting her perfectly, and even though he'd already taken about a dozen shots of her, this was the one he knew he'd want to add to the collection of photos he had of Summer. Most of his pictures of her were from middle school, when he'd gotten his first camera, high school, when he'd taken his first photography class, and college, when he'd truly perfected his craft. He was sure the image he was seeing at the moment would be one of his favorites.

He continued to observe her through his lens as she began to open her eyes and turn his way. Her gaze leveled on his just as the wind blew her curls to the side, causing the tendrils to cascade around her face. His finger took two more clicks before she changed position.

Never mind, that's the one. That's the magic shot. While he stood there, he thought about all the people he'd taken pictures of over the years. Celebrities. Models. Strangers. Friends. Out of all the accolades he'd ever received for his work, the woman looking back at him still held the number-one spot as the person he'd loved photographing the most.

Before he'd gotten his first professional camera, he'd been taking Polaroids of Summer. Before he even knew the difference between a fast and slow shutter speed, he knew how to capture her perfect facial angles and her many expressions. He'd caught the look she made when she was concentrating hard on something and was oblivious to those around her. In a way, she'd always inspired him. Still inspired him.

"Aren't you hot with your jacket zipped up so high?" he asked.

She glanced down at her jacket and slowly began unzipping it. When she removed it from her shoulders, he spotted something gold and shiny around her neck. Without thinking about it, he reached out and touched the necklace.

"Is this the locket I bought you years ago?"

"Yes," she said, touching his hand that still held her locket. "Twenty years ago, to be exact."

Twenty years... She's kept the locket for twenty years. Aiden remembered when he'd begged his dad for an early allowance to pay for it. He'd saved up for months and even done extra chores to raise money for it. A couple of times, his dad had reminded him that a 14-karat gold locket was an expensive gift to give a young girl. But Summer was never just any girl. She was his friend.

His best friend. More importantly, he'd always felt like in some way, she was *his* and he'd had to get it for her.

"Come on," she said, breaking eye contact. "Let's keep walking." They fell into a comfortable stride, neither too eager to leave the park.

"So, tell me, Summer. Besides opening up Bare Sophistication and quitting your job at the PR firm—which I think was a great idea, by the way—how has everything been these past eight years?"

She laughed. "You ask me that as if we haven't kept in contact."

"Social media, email and the occasional phone call are hardly viable ways to keep in contact considering the type of friendship we used to have."

She nodded her head. "I guess you're right."

"And our high school reunion doesn't count, either, because you ran off before I could even get to talk to you."

"An hour was all I could take of Claysville High. After seeing the exact same decorations we used to use at school dances over twenty years ago and running into Rochelle and Sam, it felt like I'd stepped into an alternate universe."

"Yeah, I know what you mean," he said with a laugh. "They both came up to me when I arrived, but the conversation was so awkward, I wasn't sure how to respond to them."

"Let me guess. Did you have some warped conversation about how they should thank you for getting them together?"

He chuckled. "Something like that. I wasn't really listening too closely. I was busy texting you to see if I could get you to come back."

"I thought you would have had your hands full with your girlfriend."

"Adriana wasn't my girlfriend during that time. We'd actually just broken up. I told you that. She was only there because she knew the producers who were shooting the documentary."

"Oh, yeah, what ever happened to that? You never told me the story, just that it wasn't going to happen"

"Apparently, Adriana thought that if we worked together we would get back together. Her producer friend pulled the plug after weeks of shooting. My company wasn't too thrilled because they were slotted to be featured in the documentary, as well."

"I can imagine. Did you really want to do a documentary?"

He thought about her question before he answered. "Yes, I did want to do it. I think I still do. At first, I thought it would be an invasion of privacy, but I'd already talked to my mom and I was ready to share my story." Truth was, he'd been more than ready to share his story. He'd already come to terms with every aspect of his life...except the part connected to the woman walking next to him.

"Have you heard from your mom?"

"Yeah, I heard from her a few months ago when I was in Greece. Apparently, she'd been assigned to shoot some photos about two hours away from where I was stationed. So I asked if she wanted to meet and she said yes."

Summer stopped walking and touched his arm. "You never told me you met up with your mom."

"That's because I didn't. I drove two hours to a restaurant she chose and she never showed."

"Typical Mia mentality. Get your hopes up just to disappoint. Again."

"Exactly. I know my mom wasn't as mean as yours. She actually wasn't mean at all. But she was hardly involved when I was a kid and when I went off to college, she couldn't wait to divorce my dad and travel the world. In some ways, I admire my mom for following her passion. But I don't understand why she couldn't do what she loves *and* be a mother. You'd think after thirty years I'd be used to the disappointment."

Neither he nor Summer had had the best female role models growing up. Their situations weren't the same, but they'd definitely bonded in their adolescence over their practically nonexistent relationships with their mothers.

"How is your dad?"

"He's good. We talk every other week, but sometimes, the conversations seem forced." He'd once had a good relationship with his father, but now their relationship was strained since his father had turned to alcohol after his mother left.

"Winter says our mom is a Vegas showgirl now. She's even the main star of the show."

Aiden glanced at her in disbelief. "Seriously?"

"I wish I wasn't."

He couldn't help but laugh. It was either laugh or get angry and he was done getting angry over his mom. "I guess both of our moms got what they wanted. A distant relationship with their children and their dream careers."

"Well, you used to always tell me that both our moms weren't cut out to be mothers. At least I think your mom did the best she could when we were younger."

"I guess you're right. She said if we were ever asked

to do a documentary together, she'd be one hundred percent in." He did truly love his mom, but he only spoke to her twice a year—on his birthday and Christmas. He hadn't seen her in over five years, and when he'd last seen her, it was only for twenty minutes in a Thailand airport.

Not only had Mia Chase left the US to travel the world, but she'd gone back to her maiden name of Meeks and was now a prolific travel photographer. She kept a low profile and most of the people she encountered didn't know that Mia Meeks was formerly Mia Chase. When his mom had told him that she'd be open to doing a documentary together, it had been heaven to his ears. He'd spent years trying to spend time with her, and a documentary together would no doubt result in them rebuilding their relationship.

Summer gently rubbed his shoulder. "Don't think too hard about it. That minor setback only means that the world wasn't ready for your documentary yet. You still have a lot of life to live. A documentary will be done on you one day and when that day comes, you'll be ready… your mom will be ready…the world will be ready."

He nodded his head and smiled. Life was funny sometimes. Aiden was usually always so positive. He never tried to dwell on the things in his life that didn't go as planned. However, in this moment with Summer, he realized he didn't have to put a positive spin on the situation. With Summer, he could just express his true feelings and know that she'd understand *exactly* how he felt.

Chapter 10

"So, almost two and a half weeks at his place and y'all haven't gotten freaky yet?" Danni asked, as they organized several boxes of lingerie that had arrived.

"Nope, we sure haven't."

"What are you waiting for? You'll only be there a few more weeks."

Summer walked over to the new lace delicates for their holiday collection. "What do you expect me to do? Just jump his bones even though we still have a lot to talk about?"

"No, I'm not saying you shouldn't talk. I'm just reminding you that you can talk and have sex at the same time."

Summer froze. "Danni, you're my girl and everything, but I didn't need to know that you like to talk dirty while having sex."

Danni shook her head as she walked over to the box Summer was consolidating. "That's not what I meant and you know it. You and Aiden can talk about whatever you need to talk about regarding your past and still find time to enjoy one another physically."

"What if we like keeping things PG?" Summer asked with a shrug. "Sometimes all you need to rekindle a friendship are some good old-fashioned one-on-one talks."

Danni gave her a blank stare. "Have you looked at *your friend* Aiden? I've never met anyone you've dated, so I don't know your type. But that man is every woman's type. You can't convince me that while you're having all those one-on-one talks, your mind doesn't wander to another one-on-one activity involving chest pressed upon chest, thighs rubbing against thighs, and mouth-to-mouth resuscitation."

"You know what's on my mind? This boutique and the upstairs boudoir studio loft," Summer said, changing the subject. "I really think the loft is coming along beautifully. I'm leaving keys with Nicole and Aaliyah, so they will check on things while we're in Michigan."

"Mmm-hmm," Danni said, raising an eyebrow. "That's fine, Summer. Go ahead and change the subject. All I'm saying is that the way he was looking at you, I was sure something would have happened by now."

Something did happen. But she couldn't tell Danni yet. Things with Aiden had gone great these past few days. So great she'd had little time to analyze the kiss they'd shared during movie night. She definitely needed to tell Danni eventually, because she needed some girlfriend advice, but they were leaving for Michigan in exactly four hours. *What if my sisters pick up on the same attraction Danni did?* She wasn't ready to talk to Winter and Autumn about Aiden and would rather just focus on all of them catching up.

What if they ask questions like Danni? What would she say? How would she react? And why would it even be an issue? She was a grown woman. No one cared if she slept with Aiden.

Summer rolled her neck to try to clear her mind. Right now, it was best to focus on the shop. If she didn't, there was no doubt in her mind that she'd freak out about all the possible scenarios that spending a weekend with her family would bring to the surface.

"Cool. Calm. Collected. Cool. Calm. Collected." Summer looked at the five wooden stairs leading to the large coffee colored door. "I just knock. After I knock, I just act cool. And calm."

"And collected," Aiden said, trailing behind her. "Is there a reason you're chanting those same three words over and over again? You've been doing so since we hopped in the rental car."

"Of course there's a reason." She glanced back at him. "My sisters can always tell if something is up with me so I have to act normal."

"And what exactly is up with you?"

She gave him a flabbergasted look. "Isn't it obvious, Aiden? Look at us!" She moved her hand back and forth between the two of them. Aiden glanced down at his jeans, coat and Timberland boots before observing her similar attire.

"What am I looking for? The fact that in Miami we were just wearing shorts and tanks, and now that we've landed in Michigan we have to dress for this chilly November weather?"

She rolled her eyes and repeated her hand movements. "Why would that be what this means?"

Aiden shrugged. "I have no idea what you mean, then."

"I agree with Aiden," Danni said, finally getting out of the car. "I was going to run inside after you opened the door, but y'all are out here fussing and I'm cold."

"We weren't fussing," Summer said. "Danni, you know how nosey my family is because you're the same way."

"Hey, I resent that."

"It's the truth. And Aiden hasn't seen them in years. We can't just walk in there like this."

Danni and Aiden glanced at each other before looking at Summer, even more confused than they'd been before.

"Like what, Summer?" Danni asked. "You're the only one who knows what you're talking about."

"No, Aiden knows, too."

"No, Aiden does not," he said.

"Why are you talking in the third person?"

"Why do you have us standing in the cold while you chant *cool, calm and collected*? Can't you chant that inside?"

"You aren't worried that my sisters and cousins will pick up on the signals?"

Aiden scrunched his head in confusion. "And what signals would that be?"

"Oh, okay," Danni said with a laugh. "I get what's going on. How about I wait at the top of the stairs while you two talk this out."

Summer walked toward Aiden to whisper in his ear. "I don't want them picking up on the sexual tension. Don't act like you have no idea what I'm talking about."

"Summer, seriously?" He raised an eyebrow. "You

think after all this time, they'll just now pick up on our attraction?"

Her eyes grew wider. "I mean, I guess we've each always thought the other was attractive, but it was different back then than it is now." Aiden tried to step around her to get to the door and she blocked him.

"Summer, I'm a grown-ass man. I'm not pretending I'm not attracted to you, and for the record, I never pretended back when we were kids, either. I'm sure your sisters knew how much I liked you."

Her mouth dropped slightly open at his words. She knew they'd had *something* going on back in the day, but Aiden had never flat-out told her that he liked her. *Did he really have to?* She'd liked him as more than a friend, too, but she hadn't said anything. *Maybe he isn't even saying he likes me like that. Maybe he still means in a friend sort of way.*

Summer groaned, annoyed at her confused state of mind. "Seriously Aiden, can we just try and focus on catching up with my family this weekend?" In the back of her head, she knew she was being irrational. Who cared if anyone picked up on their sexual tension? She kept telling herself it was no big deal, but it was. She'd never even talked to her sisters about Aiden in any fashion that wasn't the he's-just-my-friend sort of way, and they, surprisingly, hadn't acted all that concerned.

Aiden sighed. "If I agree, can we finally go inside?"

"Yes."

"Fine, I promise to *try* and act like I'm not attracted to you, and I won't even try to kiss you in front of your family."

"What about when my family isn't around?"

"I make no promises about that. We've kissed once already so it's bound to happen again."

"Wait, what? Y'all kissed?" Danni said from the top of the stairs.

"Of course Sherlock Danni is listening."

"Not my fault Aiden can't whisper," Danni said.

"Good job. You can't whisper. You just told Danni we kissed."

"What are we, five? Who cares?"

"Maybe I wanted to be the one to tell her we kissed," she said a little too loudly. *Okay, now I'm really being irrational.* Hearing herself babble about nonsense was like seeing herself trip into a pile of pig poop, unable to catch herself before she fell headfirst. At the sound of the door opening behind her, she turned around and spotted both her sisters in the doorway wearing intrigued expressions on their faces.

"Congrats. You didn't tell Danni, but you just told both your sisters." Aiden chuckled as he walked up to hug Winter and Autumn. Summer avoided eye contact with Danni as she walked up the stairs.

"You know you're wrong," Danni said, as she passed. "I talked to you this morning and traveled all this way with the two of you, and you didn't even tell me the juicy stuff?"

"I should blame you for the reason I'm so crazy right now. You put all those freaky ideas in my head."

"Blame me if you want, girlfriend, but I'm pretty sure I only mentioned what you were already thinking."

Summer was about to deny Danni's claim when they were interrupted.

"Are the two of you staying out here all night?" Both

women turned to see Jaleen Walker, who was friends with Summer's brother-in-law, Taheim.

"If it isn't the man who thinks he's God's gift to women," Danni said sarcastically. "I guess Summer's family decided to take in strays for this holiday party."

Jaleen stepped closer to Danni. "See, I knew you missed me while you've been in Miami. Couldn't wait to see me, huh, Danni?"

"Oh, please, I'm about as excited to see you as I am my gynecologist every year."

"Hmm, I can think of a few more things I'd like to have in common with your gynecologist."

Summer snickered, as she did every time Danni and Jaleen bantered.

"Sometimes you make me nauseous," Danni said, shooing Jaleen away.

"Nauseous in a good way?"

"How can you make someone nauseous in a good way?"

"Do you really want to know?" Jaleen moved his eyebrows up and down to taunt Danni.

"Eww, no. I think I'm okay."

"You'll be asking what I meant soon enough."

Danni rolled her eyes. "I doubt it."

"Anyway," Jaleen said, clasping his hands together. "There's too many married or engaged couples in here right now, so I need both you ladies to accompany me inside. As a matter of fact, I saved you both a seat at the dinner table on each side of me."

"Aren't we lucky," Danni said, batting her eyes. Jaleen only grinned.

"You guys are too much," Summer said, finally walking inside the cabin. She could spend hours listening to

Danni and Jaleen, but right now she needed to see how things were going with her family's reunion with Aiden.

She spotted him talking to three of her cousins, Malik Madden, Micah Madden and Malakai Madden, who'd texted her during the car ride over that he'd just arrived in Michigan a few hours ago. She should go over and say hi to them, but she hesitated upon seeing them laugh with Aiden. When she and her sisters used to visit her cousins in Arkansas, Aiden would sometimes accompany them on their trips. Aiden was an only child, and her aunt and uncle had six boys, so it was always a macho fest for the first few hours of their visit.

Summer made her way around the room, saying hellos to others in the cabin including Taheim, Ajay, Malik's wife, Mya, and Micah's wife, Lex. Mya and Lex were two of four members of Chicago's established Elite Events Incorporated event planning company. She'd gotten a chance to talk to both women at Winter and Taheim's engagement party, and she was glad her cousins had found such amazing women.

She neared the end of her hellos and, as it often happened whenever she was in a room, Aiden's eyes found hers. Instead of a quick glance, he gave her body a once-over. Even though she was still wearing her coat, she felt his look on every part of her body. *So much for ignoring our attraction.* She hadn't even been in the room for five minutes and she could already feel eyes observing their behavior. She broke eye contact and removed her coat before walking over to her sisters.

"Aren't you two glowing," she said, giving them both a hug.

"Thanks, sis." Winter kissed her on the cheek.

"I'm not pregnant," Autumn said. "But I agree, Winter is glowing."

Summer leaned closer to Autumn and pointed to Autumn's fiancé, Ajay. "Then you must be glowing for another reason."

Autumn blushed. "Speaking of glowing, you're looking particularly flushed right now. Am I to assume that you and Aiden finally decided to stop ignoring your attraction to one another?"

"I don't know what you're talking about."

"Oh, really," Winter said, looking from Summer to Aiden. "Did we just make up that hot eye exchange you two just had?"

"Or did we misunderstand what you said outside?" Autumn asked. "You and Aiden didn't kiss?"

Summer fidgeted with her cream-colored scarf. "We kissed, but it wasn't a big deal."

Winter glanced at Autumn before looking back at Summer. "Sweetie, you kiss your best friend of twenty-five years and you think it's no big deal?"

"No, I'm not saying that. Aiden and I haven't really talked about it."

"Well, you both may have some time to talk about it this weekend," Autumn said. "I don't know if Malik emailed you the room assignments, but you and Aiden are in the same cabin."

"No biggie. You both already know we've been living with each other for the past few weeks. We've just been catching up."

"We know, but is that your way of saying you've been prolonging the conversation?" Autumn asked.

"Maybe." Summer shuffled from one foot to the other. "Okay, yes."

Winter looked over her shoulder at Aiden. "I'm sure your conversations have been good, but I think time is running out for you to discuss the kiss with Aiden. He may be talking to the guys, but his eyes have been trained on you since you walked through the door."

Summer didn't have to look at Aiden to know Winter was right. "Yeah, they may be. But you know Aiden. He's always kept an eye on me when we're in the same room."

"Not like that, sis," Autumn said with a laugh. "That's the look of a man on a mission."

That's what I'm afraid of. It always seemed that at one time or another, Summer and Aiden had disagreed about where they should take their relationship. Should they remain friends? Should they take it one step further? Should they date or did they know too much about each other to keep the relationship casual? Or was the fact that they knew so much about each other actually the reason they should date? Questions had been stampeding through her mind since he'd walked back into her life. Then there was the scariest question of all. *Can we overcome what happened in the past or will history always linger around us?*

Summer didn't have the answers, but after weeks of spending time with Aiden, she was finally realizing that she wouldn't get any answers by avoiding the issue. She had to address the situation head-on. She stole a quick peek at him and took a deep breath. She knew what she was really afraid of, even if it was hard to admit it to herself. After all these years, maybe—just maybe—they were both at the right place at the right time.

Chapter 11

Aiden looked at the clock again before rolling onto his back. It was already 3 a.m. and he hadn't slept a wink since he got into bed at midnight. It could be the fact that Summer was in the room right down the hall and he hadn't gotten a chance to talk to her all night. She'd been acting strange around him, and he was pretty sure she'd been avoiding him.

When he initially saw the room arrangements, he'd been pleased to see that he and Summer were both placed on the first floor in one of the cabins. Much to his disappointment, Summer was sharing a bedroom with Danni. Jaleen and Malakai had the only remaining separate bedrooms on the second floor.

He hadn't lived with anyone since college, but he'd gotten used to Summer being in a bedroom right next to him. Alone. It wasn't that he'd actually acted on their attraction by knocking on her bedroom door, but he'd known she was there and that had been enough. Until recently...

Aiden had always prided himself on the level of self-control he portrayed in high-stress situations. A part of being a great photographer meant that you always had to control the photo shoot to make sure that you got a great shot. The perfect shot. He'd been suspended off the side of a South African mountain for three hours to capture a few pieces from a Johannesburg designer. He'd had a black bear interrupt a photo shoot in the Smoky Mountains and he'd still had to continue to take the shots and hope that the park rangers and the rest of the crew could handle the situation.

He'd even had to stand on the outside railing of a tall skyscraper to get the perfect shot of a suspended model wearing a chic ballroom gown. Guaranteed the model was in a more dangerous situation than he was for most of the shoot, but going over that railing and maintaining his footing required extreme confidence and willpower. Those present for the shoot warned him that he shouldn't step over the railing, but he disregarded their warnings because capturing the angle was more important to him. One wrong step could have sent him falling more than three hundred feet to his death.

All of those situations could have made him nervous, made him lose his self-control and strength of will. Yet it was the brown-haired beauty with the sultry round eyes and smooth butterscotch skin tone that was slowly breaking his resolve. It seemed the more they talked about the past and what the other had been up to the past few years, the more he couldn't get her out his mind. The more he dreamed about her. From the way she moved her mouth when she talked to the way she lightly touched his arm when she laughed at something funny he said. Even the way she'd glance at him and smile when she knew he was watching her.

Summer was his weak spot and always had been, but now it seemed she was even more of a weak spot than he'd realized. *Maybe I should see if she's up.* She probably wasn't, since everyone had gone to bed hours ago. He grabbed his phone from the charger and unlocked it to send her a text. Instead, he saw that he had several Instagram notifications that he assumed were from the photos he'd put up of the group earlier in the night.

He laughed at a few of the comments Malik and Micah had written on the photo he had posted of all the men. He laughed even harder at Jaleen's response. Although he'd just met Jaleen tonight, he was hilarious and Aiden had immediately felt like he'd known him for years.

Aiden clicked to check his notifications of pictures he was tagged in and saw a candid one that Winter had posted of everyone sometime during the night's festivities. Summer was in the photo talking to Autumn and everyone else was involved in conversation, as well, except for him. He was standing around with the guys, who were listening to something Micah was saying. But he knew he hadn't been listening. Mainly because his eyes were on Summer. *No shock there.* If he remembered correctly, this was around the time he realized she was going to avoid him all night. *She sure did a damn good job.*

He was clicking on another photo when there was a light knock on his door. He doubted Malakai, Jaleen or Danni would be knocking, so that only left one person. Since he often slept in the nude, he grabbed the cotton shirt and basketball shorts he'd placed on an armchair so that he could throw them on in the morning before breakfast.

He opened the door, but no one was there. Hoping he wasn't imagining things, Aiden stepped out the door and looked down the hall toward the stairs. He spotted Summer on the first step.

"Pssst."

He couldn't tell, since it was dark, but when she glanced at him he felt like he could sense her hesitation. "Where are you going?" he whispered.

"Back to my room."

"Why?"

She didn't say anything for a couple of seconds. "I thought you'd be sleep."

"Nope. Haven't slept at all yet."

"Why?"

Now he was silent. Luckily, he didn't have to explain and she started walking back toward his bedroom.

"Is everything okay?" he asked, shutting his door.

"Yeah, everything is fine. I just couldn't sleep and I figured if you were up, too, we could talk."

Talking wasn't exactly what he wanted to do, but he'd never turn down a moment with her.

"Sure. What do you want to talk about?" He sat on the bed and she followed.

"I don't know." She fidgeted with the cover on his bed and sat cross-legged. Aiden glanced down at her shorts before setting his eyes on her tank top. *She's trying to kill me. When did she start only wearing tank tops and shorts?* If he really thought about it, he knew that whether it be day clothes or pajamas, she'd always enjoyed wearing a simple top and shorts. Emphasis on the shorts. He just couldn't remember it getting to me like it was now.

"Did you bring any pants and long-sleeved shirts to sleep in?" he asked.

She looked down at her pajamas. "No. Why? What's wrong with what I'm wearing?"

"It's cold in this cabin."

She ran her hands over her tank and shrugged. "Danni and I have the heater on in our room, so I'm fine."

I'm not. He grabbed a pillow and placed it over his lap. Summer's eyes followed his movements, but she didn't comment on it.

"Why couldn't you sleep?" they both asked at the same time.

"You go first," she said with a laugh.

He stuck with a simple answer. "I've just got a lot on my mind." *Meaning I have you on my mind. All the time. Even when I sleep.* "What about you?"

"I'm not sure, but I think it's something I ate. I was sleeping well, but my stomach feels a little upset, so it woke me up."

"I don't think it's the rice and chicken we had for dinner. Or that delicious 7UP cake we had for dessert."

"Oh, man, wasn't it good?" Summer rubbed her stomach. "Micah's wife, Lex, makes the best desserts. You need to try her red velvet cake she's making tomorrow."

"You mean today," he said, looking at his phone again.

"That's right," she said with a laugh.

Even her half-sleepy, half-awake laugh is cute. "Your stomach is probably upset because everyone was waiting on us to eat dinner when we arrived. Then we all got to talking and didn't eat until almost 11 p.m."

"That could be it, but I've eaten late before."

"And I bet you have a restless night every time you do."

"Why do you say that?"

"Do you remember that summer right after you turned sixteen when we went to visit my grandpa Charley in

Alabama and spent the entire day picking pecans from the trees in his backyard?"

"How could I forget?" Summer asked with a smile. "After that, we made all kinds of foods with pecans. Pecan pie. Pecan cake. Pecan muffins. Pecan pancakes. Even pecan-infused chicken, which I had never heard of. It was amazing. I really miss Grandpa Charley."

"Me, too," he said, smiling at the memory of his grandfather. "Your stomach hurt the first two nights we were there, and we thought it was all the pecans. Then the next two nights, it didn't hurt at all. Since we were eating so late those first days, and around 7 p.m. those next two days, I figured I would do an experiment to see if it had to do with your eating patterns."

Summer laughed so loud, she covered her mouth. "You did an experiment on me?"

"Oh, come on," he said, joining in the laughter. "What about all those experiments you did on me growing up?"

"Point taken," she said, putting up her hands in defeat. "So, what was your experiment?"

"Well, over the next month that summer, when we were hanging out I'd take notes on the different times you ate in the evening. Then compare that to when you would tell me your stomach hurt the following morning. Just to be on the safe side, I did the experiment again that winter. I probably should have told you this years ago, but when you eat late, you should probably take something to help you digest your food. Like a probiotic or something."

Summer grew quiet and stared at him for a while before smiling. "You're pretty damn amazing, Aiden Chase. Do you know that?"

"Of course I know that," he said with a laugh.

"I never made the connection between eating at night and sleeping, and I hadn't even told my doctor about my stomach cramping at night. But I began taking probiotics to boost my immune system a couple of months ago. I usually never eat late, but I've been eating a lot later since I started preparing the shop for the grand opening. I just realized that I left my probiotics at your place in Miami. I've been so busy, I didn't even notice they were helping until tonight."

"Glad I could help," Aiden said, forcing himself to keep his eyes on hers and not her lips. Or chest. Or any other body part that would make him have to grab another pillow for his lap.

A minute later, he realized her eyes were just as bad. He could read them too well. At times, she could read his eyes even better than he could hers. It took a clever type of man to be able to hide the truth in his eyes, and although Aiden was talented, he wasn't talented enough. Either he didn't know how to hide the truth, or he didn't care if Summer saw the desire present in his eyes. Regardless, he saw the longing in hers, too. The yearning to release emotions that he had a feeling hadn't been released in a very long time.

"I changed my mind. I don't want to talk anymore," she said, breaking the silence.

He swallowed and tugged at the cotton neck of his T-shirt. "If you don't want to talk, what do you want to do?" His question was suggestive. Her response left no room for misinterpretation.

Summer lifted herself onto her knees and brought her face close to his.

"Summer," he said as a warning when she dropped her eyes to his lips. Instead of hesitating, the way he'd expected, she leaned even closer and placed each of her hands on his thighs at the edge of his basketball shorts. Her eyes danced with a challenge.

"Two lies and a truth," she said with a sly smile.

"I haven't played this since we were kids."

"Trust me," she said, as she slid her hands slightly higher under his shorts. "This won't be like when we were kids." Aiden didn't move. He couldn't move.

"I've been dreaming about your hands on my body, so that's what woke me up tonight. Sharing another passionate kiss with you seems to be the only thing on my mind lately. And I've been thinking about slipping my hands under your basketball shorts *every* time you wear them."

His mouth instantly watered at his options. *Why can't they all be true?* He would be curious about her sudden burst of boldness after she'd been avoiding him all night, if he wasn't familiar with the way Summer processed things. Once she made up her mind or came to terms with something, she didn't look back or second-guess herself. Aiden was praying this was one of those times her decisiveness was to his benefit, too.

"Um, truth. You were dreaming about my hands on your body tonight and that's what woke you up. Truth. Sharing another passionate kiss has been on your mind a lot lately." He glanced down at her hands on his thighs and contemplated changing his answer, but it was too late. "Lie. You've been thinking about slipping your hands under my basketball shorts every time I wear them."

She quirked her lips in a side smile. If she moved her hands one more inch, he'd grow even harder. Hell, just the thought was making him want to toss the pillow to the side.

"Wrong." Her hands stopped moving.

"Which one was wrong?"

"Well, yes, I've constantly been thinking about kissing you. And believe it or not, every time you go for a run and come home all hot and sweaty, I can't stop staring at your basketball shorts and imagining how they'd look off you."

"So you weren't dreaming about me tonight?"

"Oh, I was." She finally slid that last inch. "But my dream didn't wake me up. My stomach really did wake me up."

She cupped him in her hand and gasped. "You're already rock solid." Her voice was laced with desire.

"I stay rock solid around you," he said as he pulled her to him and kissed her passionately. The moment their lips touched, he moaned into her mouth. He'd been waiting for this kiss from the minute their last kiss ended.

He switched their positions so that she was securely under him, never breaking their mouths apart. With every tongue stroke, their kiss grew deeper, *bolder*. The sweet whimpers escaping from Summer's mouth sent chills down his spine. Her hands roamed under his shirt and he leaned up so she could take it off.

You both still need to talk first...

That little voice inside his head was a reminder that he and Summer had some unfinished business. But damned if he could even remember what that business was at the moment. The only thing that mattered was living in the moment and relishing the erotic way their tongues danced together.

Unable to resist tasting her sweet skin, Aiden began placing kisses along her neck and collarbone. It almost seemed unreal that just two months ago he'd awaken from a dream of her in the exact position that she was in now. His hands journeyed down to her backside and cupped both cheeks in his hands.

Definitely not dreaming right now. Summer was all woman, and right now he was ready to show her just how much he appreciated every part of her.

Breaking the kiss, he studied her eyes for any sign of regret. Seeing none, he gave her one more once-over to be sure.

"Its fine," she said, licking her lips. "I'm good." She wrapped her arms around his neck and pulled him in for another kiss. *I'll take it slow, just in case*, he thought when he realized they were venturing into uncharted territory. They'd made out before. They'd seen each other naked before. They'd even done some pretty naughty things before that they'd both admitted they hadn't regretted.

Even though they'd moved to a dance similar to the one they were about to have, they'd never tangoed quite like this. Everything was different. Life itself was different. Which meant that *this* particular moment was different.

Aiden dragged down one of the straps of her tank top until a nipple was exposed. He readily popped the nipple into his mouth and was rewarded by her upper body lifting off the bed to meet him eagerly. Minutes later, he moved to the other nipple before completely discarding her shirt and tossing it to the floor with his.

He took his time exploring her body *slowly*. He was in no rush for this moment to end. When he reached her stomach, he glanced up at her and caught the wicked smirk on her lips. She wore the look of a woman who knew what was next, but if Summer thought intercourse was the next step, she was sadly mistaken. Aiden could think of so many things he wanted to do to her body before they shared that moment.

He removed her shorts and sucked in a breath at the beautiful V-shaped haven staring back at him. She squirmed a little under his heated gaze and Aiden swore it winked at him, waiting to meet his tongue. Without waiting a second longer, he spread open her thighs and dived into her sugary treat.

"Aiden," she whispered as she bucked slightly off the bed. Gripping her butt cheeks, he brought her closer to his mouth as he dragged her down the bed so he could kneel on the floor. The change in positions gave him better access to her sweet spot, and within seconds, she was covering her mouth to conceal her moans.

This was what he'd been thinking about for years. Over a decade, even. The moment he'd learned what oral sex was, Summer had popped into his mind. She was in so many of his fantasies. So many of his memories. Even now, he was having a hard time deciphering which events of the night had allowed him to be blessed with the opportunity to taste her uninhibitedly.

"Aiden…" She bucked again. "Oh, my God." She grabbed a pillow and clamped it over her face. Of course he'd rather see her when she came, but he didn't want to break his mouth-to-haven contact to tell her so. Instead, he dived into her center even deeper when he felt her body tense. She was right on the edge and it was getting harder to keep her thighs apart.

When she let go of the pillow and brought her hands to his hair, he flicked his tongue three more times over her sensitive bud. Summer reached an orgasm quickly after, biting her fists to muffle her moans. Aiden stared at her in awe as he watched satisfaction spread to every part of her face.

He stood, lay on the bed and pulled her into his arms. "I feel like I've waited my entire life to see that look of pure ecstasy on your face."

She hugged him back and he could feel her rapid heartbeat finally start to slow down. When she glanced up at him, he saw so many emotions in her eyes, he wasn't sure which was more prominent.

"Are you okay?" he asked.

Her smile was slow and satisfied. "In this moment with you...I'm perfect." She tilted her head to his. "And now, it's my turn."

Chapter 12

When she'd envisioned how Aiden's mouth would feel on every part of her body, never had she imagined it would be so liberating. He'd made sure she felt every kiss he placed on her.

As much as she'd enjoyed having his lips pressed against her core, there was something that had been keeping her up at night. Something she just had to have.

A bare-chested Aiden was definitely a sight to behold, but a stark-naked Aiden was even better. Her fingers played with the top rim of his shorts as he lifted his hips off the bed to help her remove them. She relished the satisfaction she got from sliding the fabric over the thighs she'd been drooling over for weeks...even longer than that, when she really thought about it.

She was very well aware that he was watching her every move, and the fact that they were both so uninhibited in their nudity somehow made the moment much more intimate.

"You're beautiful," she whispered, as she journeyed up his body. When she reached his face, he pulled her down for a passionate kiss, expertly using his tongue the same way he had moments before.

Now that they'd shared several kisses, she welcomed the tingling sensations traveling throughout her body. Instead of subsiding with every touch of their lips, the burning only grew stronger. Whenever she kissed Aiden, she knew there was never just kissing involved. His expert fingers weren't only great for taking photos, painting, or creating other beautiful artistry. Kissing Aiden was like an otherworldly experience, demanding that she gave as much as she took.

Summer placed leisurely kisses down his neck, then moved her tongue across the defined crevices of his abs. Each dip of her tongue across his chiseled body brought her mouth one step closer to his shaft. Each groan into the electrified air encouraged her to push him over the edge of ecstasy.

When she reached his member, she brought her mouth over the tip and lingered there for a while before glancing up at him. His eyes were dark and dangerous, no doubt having imagined her in this position numerous times before.

"I've never done this before because I was waiting on this moment with you."

"That's funny." He gave her a sexy side smile. "I've pretty much been waiting on this moment, too."

"I don't think you understand." She moved to the other side allowing her breath to linger once more. "Do you have any idea how long I've waited to do this?" she asked holding his gaze. His Adam's apple bobbed up and down as he swallowed.

"For how long?" he asked, his usually melodic voice raspy with need.

She flicked her tongue once, then twice, just because she liked his response. "I can't place the exact date, but I can tell you that the first time I imagined sucking you into submission was in a dream." She ran her eyes lazily over his body. "And I have to say, the fantasy looked a lot like this."

With that, she closed her mouth over him and relaxed her throat as much as she could to accommodate his length. As she began moving her tongue and mouth in a pleasing rhythm, she couldn't help but watch the myriad of facial expressions he made as he got closer to the edge.

She was mesmerized by the way his abs contracted with each soft suckle and she wondered how she'd ever gone so long without seeing him like this.

"Summer," he said as a warning. "You should stop before..." His voice trailed off, but she'd gotten his message loud and clear. He didn't want to release himself into her mouth and he was on the brink of no return.

Instead of backing away, she locked her lips to him even more, enjoying the way he repeated her name over and over again. His orgasm was quick and fast as he convulsed into her mouth. She stayed with him the entire journey only releasing him to smile at the surprised look on his face.

"That was incredible," he said breathlessly, getting over the initial shock. She smiled as she nodded her head in agreement. Incredible was definitely one way to think of it. At the same time, she could think of several other ways to describe what they'd just shared. She doubted she'd ever forget this instant. *Sexiest. Moment. Ever.*

* * *

"Are you sure you're okay?"

Aiden's voice was filled with concern. Summer glanced up from her seat on the couch to look at him.

"I'm fine," she said, gently touching his forearm. She scanned the living room. Noticing that they were alone, she continued. "Last night was beautiful. You don't have to check on me every five minutes."

He gave her a soft smile. "I know I don't have to, but I can't help it. We never got a chance to talk about what happened to you back in college and I swore to myself we would talk before anything physical happened."

Summer glanced around again before standing and motioning for Aiden to follow her into the laundry room. She shut the door behind him.

"Aiden, what happened back in college was unfortunate, but I don't want to talk about it."

Her eyes focused on the vein in his neck that popped whenever he was frustrated. "Okay, I get it, but I really don't think it's healthy for you to hold in your feelings."

"I'm not holding in my feelings," she said, a little louder than she'd wanted. "You can't get upset at me for not wanting to talk about bad circumstances. Shit happens every day and people deal with their problems. The world doesn't stop because something unlucky happens."

"Unlucky?" He studied her eyes and stepped closer to her. "Summer, after all these years, you still can't talk to me about this?"

She averted her eyes to the window momentarily getting lost in the stillness of the lake. They'd had such a beautiful night, and now he had to ruin it by bringing up the past. *Her* past.

She turned back to Aiden. "After all these years, you can't let it go? I was unlucky. End of story."

His face tensed, but his voice remained calm. "Unlucky is what you call it when you miss your plane or when you fall down the stairs. Not when you're sexually assaulted."

She cringed at his statement. At times his directness was too much to handle. "Listen, when you called me four years ago and asked me to talk to that psychiatrist you'd met, I went to her. It helped."

"But you stopped going to her after two sessions."

"Because I didn't have anything left to say about the situation. Did you know that one out of five women are sexually assaulted? Do you know what that means?"

"That there are lot of women who can relate to your story?"

"Yes, that's true, which means what happened to me could happen to anybody."

"But it didn't happen to anybody." His voice got lower. "It happened to you and until you actually talk about it and realize that it wasn't your fault, you'll never be able to heal from it."

Summer closed her eyes and started counting in her head to try to ease the building tension in her temples. *I can't believe he's trying to take me back there.* She considered herself the type of person who could overcome anything and based on the obstacles she'd already had to face in life, she'd proved that fact to be true. Yet Aiden didn't seem to care about how much she'd grown. All he cared about was making his point, despite how she may feel about it.

"How the hell would you know if I've healed or not?" she yelled, her anger rising. "You weren't around when it happened and you weren't there for me right after it happened, either!" Aiden's jaw twitched, but he didn't say anything.

"You'll always be there for me, right? That's what you said." She felt the tears form in the back of her eyes. "When your grandfather passed away, I was there. When your mom left without a backward glance, I was there. When your dad started drinking and you had to take him to rehab, I was there. For every situation, you called me and within minutes or hours, I was by your side helping you through it. Don't get me wrong, I know you were there for me, too, when my mom left and when I was sad, and happy that my dad was moving back to France to follow his dream. You were there for me for a lot of other times, too, so I'd never discount that. But you weren't there this particular time, so if I don't want to talk about it, that's my prerogative."

However, now that she'd started her outburst, she couldn't stop. "I understand that we went to different colleges, but our schools were only a few hours apart from each other. You weren't there when I was going through the worst experience of my life and even after, I drove all the way to your school for help. For guidance. For support while I tried to figure out why it had happened and what I should do. Even when I got there, you weren't at your campus apartment and your roommate said he thought you'd gone out of town. So I called. And called. And called. But you didn't return one call that night, or even that week. Or the next."

She finally lowered her voice. "Ask yourself this question, Aiden. Do you want to talk about what happened so badly because you truly think I need to heal? Or do you want to talk about the situation because you're the one who needs to recover?"

His eyes held hers, but they were void of emotion. Whenever Aiden really got upset about something, he would eventually hit a point where he grew eerily silent... like he was now.

The more she looked at him, the worse she felt. She hated fighting with Aiden. Especially when he really had always been her rock. *Except that one time...*

Instead of standing there and waiting for him to talk, Summer opened the door and walked briskly to the bathroom at the end of the hall. She closed and locked the door, just in case he got any ideas of following her in there. Between last night and this morning, her emotions were in a ball of mass confusion.

Don't you dare cry! Don't you dare shed another tear over this! Opening her eyes, she leaned over the sink and glanced at her reflection in the bathroom mirror. Her family had a big outing today, and even though she didn't want to go, she knew she'd have to or her sisters would worry.

She turned on the faucet on splashed some warm water across her face. Time for her to do what she did best...pretend that everything was okay.

"We're here early, so I have an idea," Malakai Madden said to the group. "I know my brothers already talked to the men who are in love with my cousins, but I need to check them out for myself."

Summer glanced at Autumn and Winter, who rolled their eyes. Malakai had already talked to both men plenty, so she assumed he just wanted to have a guys-only talk. They were at a beautiful Michigan winery that had several paths for exploring the property's forest full of brilliant ginger, crimson and buttery-colored trees. Michigan was one of the most beautiful places she'd seen in the late fall.

"So, how about all the ladies head down the first path and the men head down the second? We'll meet in an hour for the official wine tour."

Everybody nodded their heads in agreement. The women immediately began walking toward a beautiful row of trees they'd seen when they'd pulled into the gravel lot of the winery. Summer caught Aiden's eye, and instead of looking upset at how she'd unfairly yelled at him, he gave her a sincere smile. She wouldn't blame him if he stayed mad at her, but she was glad that he didn't seem to want to fight any more than she did. Summer mouthed that she was sorry and in return, he mouthed that he was, too.

When they'd been walking for twenty minutes, Summer felt an overwhelming urge to talk to her sisters. She wasn't sure why she felt the need to talk to them now, but for whatever reason, putting on a facade and pretending that nothing was wrong wasn't something she wanted to do today. They'd both asked her if she was okay earlier.

Summer pulled Danni to the side. "Can I ask you a favor?"

"Sure! What do you need?"

"I have to talk to Winter and Autumn about something important. Can you continue walking with Lex and Mya while I pull them aside for twenty minutes?"

"Of course I can." Danni gave her a quick hug. Danni hadn't asked what was wrong, but Summer assumed that she must've heard a little of the argument between her and Aiden that morning in their cabin. "We'll keep walking for about ten or fifteen minutes. Then we'll circle back."

"Sounds good." Summer led Winter and Autumn to a wooden bench a couple of feet away.

"What's wrong?" Winter asked. "The look on your face is worrying me."

Summer took a deep breath. "I need to tell you both something very important. It's about a situation that happened to me in college."

"What happened?" Autumn asked.

Now that it was time for her to be honest with them, she was nervous. She'd kept the secret from them for so long. *Just tell them what happened. Just come out and say it.*

"While I was away at college, I was slipped a date rape drug while I was at a party and sexually assaulted later that night."

Autumn's hand flew to her mouth and Winter's eyes immediately watered. Summer took another deep breath and continued. "The only reason I know I was sexually assaulted is because I woke up the next morning with my panties torn and I was extremely sore in my vaginal area. I immediately realized that I knew where I was. I knew the apartment and the room, and couldn't believe that not only was I assaulted, but it was by someone I knew and trusted at school."

Autumn covered her eyes with her hands and Summer assumed it was to stop herself from crying and to regain composure.

"Why didn't you tell us when it happened?" Winter asked, not masking her tears.

"You both were upset that Dad was moving to France, and even though we were all eventually happy for him, I didn't want to stress you both out any more. I also didn't know how to deal with what had happened."

"When did it happen?" Autumn asked.

"Eight years ago…during my senior year."

Winter scrunched her forehead in thought. "Around the same time you and Aiden stopped being friends?"

Instead of answering, she nodded her head. Autumn placed her hand on Summer's arm.

"Sis, Winter and I always said we wouldn't ask you why your friendship ended with Aiden after the first time when you were so upset we asked. But I'm asking now. What happened?"

Summer sighed as she looked up into the colorful trees. "Aiden wasn't there for me when everything happened. It was right around the time he was starting his career and had gotten the internship at Palmer Lane. He was in a taxi heading to the London airport. I'd called numerous times and I'd even driven up to his university. I didn't find out where he was or why he hadn't returned my calls until more than a week later, and by that time, I'd felt like I'd been to hell and back."

There was so much more to the story and how it had all unfolded that night, but Summer didn't want her sisters to be too overwhelmed.

"Almost two weeks after it happened, Aiden drove to my campus apartment while I was in class. My roommate let him in and although my roommate didn't know the entire story, she was so angry about what she did know that she told Aiden a few things. When I got home, he was furious."

"Knowing how protective he is of you, I can imagine how upset he was," Winter said.

"Upset is an understatement," Summer said, as she

stopped looking at the trees and turned to look back at her sisters.

Autumn looked at her with concern. "There's more to the story, isn't there, Summer?"

Summer fidgeted with her coat. "Yes."

"Do you want to tell us the rest?" Winter asked.

Summer thought about the details she'd left out. With the exception of the physiatrist that Aiden had begged her to see, she hadn't talked to anyone about all the particulars.

"There is more to the story," Summer said. "But I'm still trying to come to terms with the fact that after all this time I've told you both what happened. Is it okay if we talk about the rest at another time?"

"Sure," Autumn said, leaning to give her a hug. "Can I give you some advice, though?"

"Sure you can."

Autumn glanced at Winter before speaking. "I know that you and Aiden have always said that you're only friends, but Winter and I have always known that you two are much more than that. Sometimes, a situation that you may feel has only impacted your life has actually impacted those around you, as well. My guess is that Aiden has never forgiven himself for not being there for you. He's always worn his heart on his sleeve…except when it came to conflict. We didn't have an easy childhood, but he didn't, either. Some would never guess that, because he's charming, loyal to a fault, open and honest, so they think they know the real Aiden Chase. The carefree guy who happens to be an accomplished photographer. But we know differently."

Winter placed her hand on Summer's other arm. "Sweetie, whether you see it now or not, he loves you and you love him. You both have always put so much stress on your friendship. But I think it was probably more exhausting for you and Aiden to put on the façade of being just friends than to give in and see what would happen if you dated. There's a reason he's back in your life. Why not see what happens when you both stop thinking so much and just start living."

Summer nodded her head in agreement, letting her sisters' words soak in. "I'm really trying not to think so hard, but this morning we got into a huge fight about the past. I even said some things that I wish I could take back, now that I'm really putting things into perspective."

"It will work out," Autumn said. "But you have to forgive Aiden for not being there."

"I do forgive him," Summer said, truly meaning the words.

Autumn studied her eyes once more. "I believe you, but he isn't the only one you need to forgive. You need to forgive yourself, too. Winter and I can wait to hear the entire story when you're ready, but the sooner you realize that whatever happened wasn't your fault, either, the better you will feel and the better your relationship will be with Aiden."

"Autumn's right," Winter added. "You and Aiden have already wasted years apart over a horrible decision that the man who assaulted you made that night. Sis, in order for you to truly heal you cannot let that situation have power over any aspect of your life."

"I know you both are right, and trust me, I didn't let that event define my life." She exhaled and wiped the tears that were starting to fall. "Although I wish it hadn't, it did affect my relationship with Aiden. It even affected my relationship with myself." She glanced up at the trees again as the tears continued to fall.

"Dammit, even now I get pissed off thinking about it. Guys, I knew the man who assaulted me. I think what really makes me angry is the fact that someone I knew could break my trust and not give a damn about what he did to my body or the fact that he knew I didn't want it. I didn't even report it because I was embarrassed at the time and heartbroken that my trust had been destroyed. Add to that, me not being able to contact Aiden who was my support system at the time. Luckily for me, the jerk who assaulted me graduated that winter. But for that entire last semester and a couple years after, I felt numb to so much. I'd graduated summa cum laude. I'd landed my dream PR job. I'd found an awesome Manhattan condo. But I still felt numb. When I saw you both, or when I visited Dad during that time, I pretended to be fine, but I wasn't."

She looked at Winter and Autumn, who were crying along with her. "You both know I'm not a weak-minded person, but I was in such a bad head space. Aiden and I fought this morning because he said I needed to talk about it and that holding it in wouldn't help me heal. Of course I snapped at him, but now that I've thought about what he said and I've talked to both of you, I realize that talking about it, doesn't make me weak…it just makes me human."

Winter gave her a tight hug and Autumn joined right in. As they stood there in the midst of such a beautiful place, talking about such an ugly subject, Summer realized something for the first time. After years of hoping for an emotional breakthrough, she was finally experiencing one. She was healing in a place that she hadn't even known was broken.

She touched the locket around her neck and smiled as she thought about another revelation. She may have pushed Aiden away all those years ago, but she'd never stopped wearing the locket he got her. So in his own special way, he'd still been right there with her, fighting by her side.

Chapter 13

Aiden bit into a piece of wheat toast as he glanced around the main cabin for the third time that morning.

"Looking for Summer?" Malakai asked with a knowing smile.

"Um, no. I was actually just wondering where all the women were."

Malakai looked unconvinced. "Malik and Micah took their wives into town to do some shopping before we all leave this evening."

Jaleen sat down across the table from Aiden. "I think Taheim and Ajay went to town with Winter and Autumn, too. They're checking out a bar that they're thinking of investing in."

"So the three of us and Danni and Summer are the only ones at the cabins right now?"

Jaleen took a swig of orange juice. "Yup. They left all us single folks here so they can do that lovey-dovey crap without anyone complaining."

"You're the only one who's been complaining all weekend," Malakai said with a laugh.

"He's right," Aiden added. "Every time any of them kissed at the winery yesterday, you made kissy noises."

"Hey, y'all don't know what I go through. Neither of you live in Chicago with them."

"I can imagine," Malakai said. "Actually, when I was at my parent's house in Arkansas for the Fourth of July this summer, Malik and Micah were all over Mya and Lex. My other brothers and I could barely watch them."

"That's nothing," Jaleen said. "When Taheim and I first moved into our condo building, we gave each other a spare key, just in case we got locked out or something. I used to be able to stop by Taheim's place anytime I wanted, but now, I never know how I'll find them. I get that Winter designs lingerie, but damn, do they have to go at it like animals before every guys' night? Especially when guys' night is at Taheim's place."

Malakai choked on his water. "Man, Winter's my cousin, so that's way too much information."

"Sorry," Jaleen said with a laugh. "But it got so bad, I decided to give my key back."

"I probably would have done the same thing," Aiden said, glancing at the front door one more time.

"She's not here."

Aiden turned to Malakai. "I know she isn't."

"If you know, why are you looking around the room and watching the front door?" Malakai asked.

"No reason."

"What's going on between you and Summer, anyway?" Jaleen asked.

"That's exactly what I want to know," Malakai said. "He's been avoiding the topic all weekend."

Aiden looked at Jaleen and Malakai, wondering how much he should tell them. Jaleen didn't know about the type of relationship he had with Summer, but Malakai definitely knew how close they'd been. He'd known Malakai and the rest of Summer's family for about as long as he'd known her.

"Nothing serious is going on. We're just rekindling our friendship."

"Do we look stupid?" Jaleen asked, taking a bite of his bacon. "Y'all look like you're rekindling more than just a friendship."

Malakai crossed his arms over his chest. "My sentiments exactly." Aiden observed Malakai. He knew that tone. Malakai wanted a straight answer and as Summer's cousin—and as someone Aiden considered an old friend—he felt it only fitting to tell him the truth.

"Okay, in all honesty, I can't even remember the last time I looked at Summer as only a friend. For so long now, I've been interested in being much more than friends. But we've both gone through a lot and back in the day, she didn't want to ruin our friendship by dating, so we didn't. Now that we've reconnected, we really have been working on the friendship part of our relationship."

"Trust me, bro, I think you've resolidified the friendship," Jaleen said. "And there is nothing friendly about the way you two look at each other. You and Summer look like two lions who start off scrapping for the same piece of meat, and then that fight turns into a playful competition. Soon the meat is forgotten. But just as you remember the meat and think you've distracted the other lion, giving you a chance to grab the meat, you realize you want to share it. Then you're pissed at yourself because you never want to share the meat."

Aiden glanced at Malakai before both men gave Jaleen an amused look.

"Are we talking about me and Summer or something else entirely different?"

"Isn't it obvious?" Jaleen asked with a shrug. "We're talking about you and Summer."

Malakai gave Jaleen a puzzled look. "You lost me somewhere between playful competition and sharing meat."

"Oh, come on, you both know what I mean."

"Not really," Malakai said with a laugh. "What I do know is that Aiden and Summer have been fighting their attraction ever since we were kids."

Malakai turned his attention back to Aiden. "I don't know what's going on between the two of you or why you disconnected for a few years, but I do know that my brothers and I have always appreciated the fact that Summer had you as a friend."

"Thanks, Malakai. I'm glad I have her in my life, too."

"You're welcome. The connection the two of you have is only yours to define." Malakai finished eating what was left on his plate. "Even though I hope you and Summer do end up together, don't think I won't kick your ass if you hurt her."

Aiden laughed. "Threat received loud and clear."

"Man, not you, too," Jaleen said. "You shouldn't even be at the single man's table the way Summer has your nose so wide open."

Aiden didn't even bother responding to Jaleen. Especially when he continued with his lions fighting over meat story.

"I was hoping I'd find you here."

Summer glanced over her shoulder at Aiden. "I probably shouldn't be sitting by the lake in forty-five-degree weather, but it looked so beautiful that I couldn't help myself."

Aiden sat down next to her on the dock. "The nature is really beautiful around here, and lakes always relax you when you have a lot on your mind."

She grinned. "Guess I'm a creature of habit."

"Only when it comes to certain things."

His arm brushed against hers, and even through their coats, she could feel the heat emanating from his body. Within minutes, their feet were swaying together in unison.

"I'm really sorry about how I acted yesterday." She turned her head to him. "I overreacted and I definitely could have handled the situation differently."

"I'm sorry, too." He gave the hand nearest to him a gentle squeeze. "I never should have tried to force you to talk about something you weren't ready to talk about. Even though you were speaking out of anger, I think you were right. I was pushing you more for my benefit than yours."

"You were right, too. I just didn't want to hear it yesterday or any of the other times you tried to get me to open up. But we do need to talk. I owe it to myself and to you to discuss it."

Two ginger-colored leaves that had been floating a foot apart were pushed together by a light ripple in the water. It almost felt like a sign for her to continue.

"I'm not going to pretend that I'm completely over what happened eight years ago, but over the past few years I've really come to terms with the fact that even though I can't change the past, it doesn't define me and never will. I've only dated one person seriously since college. His name was Rashad. I think I told you about him in a few emails."

"You did."

"I thought so." She glanced down at their intertwined fingers. "Through the course of me dating him, I was able to learn even more about myself. One of the things I learned in my post-college relationship was that I truly did have the ability to trust a man again. Rashad was a good man, and even though I never told him what happened in college, he knew it was something serious and he remained patient with me without even knowing the core of my trust issues. I'm going to say this now because I want to make sure you hear me loud and clear."

She took a deep breath and looked Aiden directly in his eyes. "I'm sorry that ending our friendship senior year hurt you, because I never meant to do that. It broke my heart to know that I was the reason we had to distance ourselves. However, whether you understand my decision or not, I needed to distance myself from you during that time because there were so many emotional obstacles I had to overcome and I couldn't do that with you by my side."

He studied her eyes. "I could have helped you through the issues."

"You could have, but I didn't see it that way at the time. I needed to stand on my own two feet." She looked back out at the water. "Aiden, being sexually assaulted by someone you don't know is devastating. But being sexually assaulted by someone you do know…someone you trust and love…is a pain I wouldn't wish on anyone."

"I could kill him for what he did to you."

"I know, but then you'd be in jail and I'd be without you in my life forever."

They were silent for a few seconds and she could feel the frustration in the air around them.

"Eight years ago, you were so angry and I'd been so distraught that I didn't get a chance to tell you everything. I'm ready to tell you what happened the morning I woke up. I don't remember much from before that, but I do remember when I woke up," she said after a while.

Aiden took a deep breath. "Okay."

"Will you be able to handle it?" She was starting to realize that Autumn was right. It may be her burden to bear, but it definitely affected those close to her, as well.

"Yes, I'm ready to hear the rest of the story."

Eight years ago...

Summer awoke and blinked her eyes several times until her blurry vision cleared. Her hand immediately flew to her throbbing head. *What's going on?* The room she was in was pretty dark, but she could tell she was on a bed next to a wall.

She waited until her eyes adjusted to the darkness. *I know this room.* Some things looked a little out of place, but she definitely knew the room. A glow from the corner got her attention. *Jake's room. I'm in Jake's room, in his bed.* The light from the bathroom door was turned on and she could hear water running. She assumed Jake was taking a shower. *Something isn't right.*

Slowly she lifted the bedsheet, immediately realizing that she was naked beneath the covers. She quickly rose from the bed, panicked by the thought of what may have happened. She opened the blinds so that the streetlights could shine through and found her panties on the floor, ripped at the side.

No. No. No. No. No. This couldn't be happening. She refused to believe it. *Okay, Summer, just calm down. Find the rest of your clothes first. Then figure out what happened.* As she found her clothes and got dressed as fast as she could, she tried her best to ignore the sore ache between her legs. An ache that made it all too clear that her worst fears had come true.

She was so wrapped up in trying to remember what had happened before she'd awakened that she didn't hear the bathroom door open.

"Why are you dressed, angel face?" Jake said with a towel wrapped around his waist.

"Don't call me angel face."

"Why not?" He started walking toward her, but Summer stopped him. "Don't you dare come near me."

"Oh, come on, Summer. After such a great night, how can you ruin it by acting all weird?"

"How can you even stand there and act like you didn't do anything wrong?" Her voice rose higher with every word she said. "Why can't I remember what happened last night and why was I naked when I woke up?"

"Don't you remember?" he asked, seemingly unaffected by her voice rising. "You said you had a birthday present for me, and since we were also celebrating our five-month anniversary, I guess you decided to make it extra special. And it was, angel face, it really was."

Summer closed her eyes and tried her best to remember what had happened, but she couldn't remember anything after being at a bar celebrating Jake's birthday with his friends and her roommate. She hadn't even drunk much. She had a test to study for, so she'd only had a glass of wine. *And whatever that drink was that Jake brought you when he arrived at the bar with his friends.*

"What did you do to me?" Tears burned her eyes, but she refused to cry in front of him. "I always remember everything and I'm not a heavy drinker. You drugged me, didn't you?"

"You better watch what you say. I didn't drug you and it's ridiculous that you think I would. What's wrong, Summer? Can't imagine having sex with me? I spent two years chasing behind you before you finally agreed to go out with me, and then after five months, we finally had sex. What's the big deal?"

She tried her best to control her anger, but she was slowly coming unglued. Jake wasn't just her boyfriend. He'd been her science partner two years ago and a good friend ever since then. "It's a big deal if the sex isn't consensual, Jake."

He took two steps toward her, his eyes full of anger. "I don't know who you think you are, but you better watch your mouth making accusations like that. Are you mad that you slept with me? So Aiden is the only one who can hit that?"

"Aiden is just my friend and he has nothing to do with this."

"Yes, he does. He's the third person in our relationship, since he comes here to visit you every other weekend. I was standing outside your apartment when you told your roommate that you'd talked it over with Aiden and you thought it was best that we break up, but you were going to wait until after my birthday. Maybe next time you'll close your window when you're talking crap about somebody."

Summer stared at him unable to believe that she'd dated the guy standing before her. The guy she'd thought of as a friend before they started dating. She thought about the signs she'd ignored. Recently, he'd been acting possessive and would do crazy things like show up to her girls' nights or pop up at a study group if another guy was present.

She'd already stopped staying at his place because she got tired of waking up and finding him watching her intently. It was even creepier when he'd pop up places and not make his presence known. Luckily, she was observant, so she often spotted him. She even caught him texting her guy friends on her phone one day, when he forgot to erase a few of the messages he'd sent.

"Jake, what did you do," she said as a statement rather than a question. She already knew what he'd done. Even though she didn't remember what happened, it wasn't consensual. She'd been sexually assaulted by a guy who'd claimed to care about her, and even worse, he seemed to be satisfied that he'd finally had sex with her in such a horrific way.

"Don't give me that look. When you begged me to have sex, did you think I wouldn't do it just because I knew you wanted to break up with me? No chance, angel face, I've been waiting two years for this moment."

Instead of staying in his apartment and allowing the situation to get any worse, she grabbed her purse off the floor and rushed out of there. She didn't stop running until she'd gotten to her apartment. It may have been five o'clock in the morning, but when she walked in, her roommate was up and on her computer.

"Oh, my God, Summer, I was so worried about you. You never spend the night at Jake's place."

She'd only lived with her roommate for a couple of months, but they'd gotten pretty close. "Christine, what happened last night?"

"At the bar?"

"Yes."

"Well, after I came back from the bathroom, Jake's friends told me you both had left. I tried your phone several times and you didn't answer, so I finally left and went home."

Summer opened her purse and spotted the missed calls on her phone. "So I left with Jake before one in the morning?"

"Yes,"

"What about the drink Jake brought for us? Do you remember what it was?"

"Um, I'm not sure. Something with tequila in it, I think. I know you and I don't go to bars too much, but after one glass of wine and one drink, you seemed to be feeling pretty good. I didn't think you'd leave me at the bar with Jake's friends, though."

One. Two. Three. Four. Five... Summer began counting in her mind as she tried to calm her rapid heartbeat. "Chris, I didn't willingly leave with Jake."

Summer was still counting in her mind as Christine's eyes raked over her from head to toe, no doubt realizing how disheveled her clothing and hair appeared.

"Summer, what are you saying?" Christine rushed to Summer's side. "Did Jake force himself on you? Do you need me to drive you to the hospital? Do we need to call the police? What happened, Summer?"

"Twenty-one. Twenty-two. Twenty-three." She began counting out loud as Christine threw questions at her that she didn't know how to answer. Summer walked into her bedroom to change into jogging pants and a T-shirt, but Christine continued asking her what had happened when she returned. Summer absentmindedly touched the locket around her neck as she thought about what she needed to do.

"I need to go see Aiden. I need to go now." She rushed out the door, ignoring her roommate's plea for her to stay. As soon as she got into her car, she called Aiden's cell and got his voicemail. She called three more times with no answer and assumed he was still sleeping. It didn't matter that she had a three-hour drive ahead of her. The only person who could help her make sense of the situation was Aiden. The only person who could help her was Aiden.

Chapter 14

She came to see you, but you weren't there for her.
Words that he wished weren't true haunted his state of
mind the more Summer talked.

"During that drive to your campus apartment, I tried
my best not to let my anger consume me. But it was use-
less. I was so angry, and not just at Jake. I was angry
because I felt like I'd ignored the signs of what type of
person he truly was."

"Don't do that," Aiden said, reminding himself to
breathe. "You can't blame yourself for what he did."

"I don't blame myself now, but in order for you to
truly understand, I need to tell you how I felt back then.
Eight years ago, I did blame myself because I felt like I'd
spent my life being able to spot people who had a hidden agenda, and somewhere along the line I'd missed the
signals with Jake. Until it was too late."

With all the strength he had, he continued to look her
in the eyes as she continued her detailed account of what
had happened. His anger level had been at an all-time

high the entire time Summer spoke about what happened the morning she awoke in Jake's room.

It wasn't just the fact that he was dealing with his own guilt that made him angry. It was the fact that every time he'd driven to her school and seen her with Jake, he'd known something was off about the guy. But at the time, Aiden had been trying to fight his own attraction for Summer, so he'd chalked up some of his feelings to jealousy.

"Can I ask you something?"

Unlike previous times they'd tried to discuss this topic, her eyes didn't seem guarded today. "You can ask me anything."

Just ask her, Aiden. You have to ask her. "That night with Jake…" His voice trailed off.

"Just ask me," she said when he didn't continue.

He held her gaze, trying to muster up the courage to ask his question. "That night with Jake…were you a virgin before that night?"

Summer didn't answer his question. She didn't have to. The tears falling down her cheeks were all the answer he needed. All these years, he'd suspected it, but he'd never asked her eight years ago. Looking back, he wasn't even sure he could have handled her response.

"I was." She finally broke their eye contact. "It wasn't really anything I'd thought about, so when Jake brought up the subject after one month of dating, I told him that I was saving myself for marriage. Looking back, I think I did that because I knew I didn't want to have sex with him." Her voice cracked slightly. "I knew he wasn't the person I wanted to lose my virginity to, but he took my decision away from me and stole what was never intended to be his."

Aiden leaned over and wiped the tears under her eyes. "I'm so sorry I wasn't there for you." He'd explained what had happened as many times as she'd listen, but he had to explain it again.

"The week before you drove down to my school, I'd learned that I'd been chosen as one of five students to intern at Palmer Lane and spend two weeks in London. I know I've told you this before, but there's no excuse for me not telling you about the opportunity. I'd been meaning to tell you when I'd visited you that weekend, but we'd gotten into a fight about your relationship with Jake and when I'd left your apartment, I realized that the real person at fault was me. I was the one who hadn't told you how I felt about you until it was too late. I promised myself that day I left that I'd give you some space and time to make your own decisions. You and I had always been so close…our lives so intertwined."

"I heard everything you were trying to tell me that day," Summer said, running her hand over his. "It hadn't been too late and when you'd walked into my apartment that day and kissed me with so much passion and promise, the mere thought about finally being together after all those years had caused so much emotion to swell in my heart. Looking back, I think it's because I wanted a relationship with you just as much. But I had to end my relationship with Jake first." Her hand stopped moving over his as she glanced back out to the water.

"Ending our relationship wasn't the only thing Jake heard that night he eavesdropped outside my living room window." Her tears had slowed, but her eyes were still filled with haunted memories of a situation that neither of them could change. "When my roommate went to the bathroom, I touched the locket you gave me, like I always do. I'm sure you've seen me rub it many times, even while we've been sitting on the dock. Occasionally I'll even talk aloud, which is what I was doing the day Jake had heard me. He and I had gotten into arguments about my relationship with you in the past, just like you and I had about him. When I held the locket that day, I told myself that in my heart I knew you were the only one for me. I knew you were the only man I'd ever truly wanted to be with."

Aiden dropped his head, trying to stop the hurt and regret that crawled throughout his body and inched through his heart. "I'm so sorry," Aiden said softly. "I'm sorry that I got your calls at the airport and didn't answer. Even though my phone service didn't work in London, I'd received your urgent emails to call you and I chose to ignore them."

"Aiden, I understand what you were doing. Like you said, we were so wrapped up in each other's lives and we'd never gone more than two weeks without seeing one another. If you think about how many hours, months and years we've spent together, it made sense that we would eventually need a break as our feelings grew stronger. Especially when we couldn't seem to figure it out back then."

Aiden dragged his fingers over his face, pissed that he could have handled things much differently. "There hasn't been a day I haven't regretted pushing you away and not being there for you at a time when you needed me the most."

"You'd planned on distancing yourself for two weeks. I'm the one who distanced myself from our friendship, which ended up lasting for years." Summer placed her head on his shoulder as they both looked out at the lake.

"I finally told my sisters what happened. Not everything, but most of it."

Aiden wrapped an arm around Summer and gently pulled her closer to him. "I'm glad you told them. And thank you for telling me the rest, too."

"You're welcome." Summer scooted closer to him on the dock. "You were right. Talking to those close to me about this is what I really needed to start healing the piece of my heart that still held on to what happened. I'm not going to pretend that I'm not still angry about it, but that situation doesn't define me any more than the issues I have with my mother do." She lifted her head to look at him.

"My situation doesn't define you, either, Aiden. I know you're an amazing man. I think we can both agree that the deeper our friendship grew and the more we realized we were much more than friends, the harder it got for us to just be us. There is so much of me I see in you, and so much of you I see in me, that we'd blurred the lines between friends and lovers in a way that had consumed every part of us. Now we're older. Wiser. And I now understand what I'd failed to understand all those years ago."

Aiden studied her eyes, failing to keep his own emotions at bay. She was right. He couldn't remember a time when he didn't look in the mirror at himself and instead of seeing his own reflection, saw a combination of his and hers. "What do you understand now that you didn't then?"

Her eyes briefly dropped to his lips. "It may have taken me years, but now I finally understand that the makeup of the long-lasting relationships that we read about in books or see in movies is that the couple builds a solid foundation. Whether it be a foundation that's built after they fall for one another, or one that was built before they even began to fall—like ours—the fact that a good foundation is needed is the core of their success. We have the ingredients needed for a strong relationship, and we always have had that."

As Aiden sat on that dock with Summer, he realized that this was the first time in eight years that neither one of them was hiding from the truth. They may have felt broken at times, but never defeated. "Are you saying that you're ready for us to actually enter a relationship? And I'm not talking about the type of relationship where I can't kiss you in public or around your family. I'm talking about the type of relationship in which I get to claim you as mine and me as yours."

She smiled as she leaned into him a little more. "I'm game if you are."

"Baby, I've been game for decades," he said, before he leaned down and placed a soft kiss on her lips. The kiss quickly deepened into something so much sweeter than it had before. This kiss felt unrestricted, free of regret from the past.

There was so much more Aiden wanted to tell Summer. So many more emotions he needed to release. However, he knew they needed time because too much had been discussed today.

When he felt like she was ready, he'd tell her what was in his heart. Summer wasn't just his friend. She wasn't just the woman who was now his girlfriend. She was the woman he was deeply and unconditionally in love with. She was the woman who'd stolen his heart so long ago, he didn't remember a time when it wasn't hers.

Chapter 15

"Summer, everything looks amazing," Aaliyah said, as she glanced around the loft that was staged for a boudoir photo shoot. Everything was coming along beautifully, and with the furniture in place and the lingerie on the racks, it was actually starting to look like a real lingerie boutique.

"It really does," Nicole added. "I can't wait for the photo shoot tomorrow. I'm anxious to see Aiden in action."

"Me, too," Summer said before turning to Danni. "Did we get a final tally of how many models will be arriving?"

"We'll have five models in total, each representing a different ethnic group."

"Fantastic." The women all agreed to meet back at the shop tomorrow morning. Summer walked the women out and locked the door before glancing at the clock. Aiden was due to arrive at the boutique in thirty minutes to set up his camera equipment and make sure everything was in place to shoot photos for his exhibit.

Tomorrow would also give the ladies a chance to see how well they worked together and to iron out any procedures before they started to announce that Bare Sophistication would also have a boudoir studio.

She dimmed the lights on the first level of the shop and walked back toward the stairs leading to the loft. When she was almost to the first step, the most recent lingerie set that Winter had shipped over was hanging on the rack. The deep purple and black set was one of Summer's favorites. The satin and lace combination on the bodice was breathtaking, and the matching boy shorts added to the overall look. Summer planned on recommending that customers pair it with sheer black thigh highs and heels of their choice.

Too bad I can't wear this for Aiden. Ever since they'd gotten back from Michigan a few days ago, he'd kept things pretty PG-13. When Summer had asked why, he'd claimed that after such an emotional talk—not to mention one of the hottest experiences of her life—he wanted to make sure she was ready. Well, she had news for him. She was more than ready, and *waiting* was no longer a word she wanted in her vocabulary.

"This is why they invented sexy toys," she said to herself. She'd never been into toys, but she still had ten days in Aiden's home. If she was going to get through it in one sex-deprived piece, she'd have to do something to relieve the ache she constantly felt when around him.

She placed the lingerie back on the rack and froze. Looking at the seductive piece before glancing down at the black heels she'd chosen to wear today, she suddenly had a plan. She just hoped it worked. She pulled her phone out of her back pocket and texted Aiden that she was leaving a spare key to the shop under the outside welcome mat.

She grabbed the lingerie off the rack and raced up the stairs. Aiden may be fine with kissing until they were blue in the face, but as wonderful as his lips felt on hers, she wanted more. She *needed* more.

Aiden glanced at the text message again. "Why can't she just open the door?" he asked aloud as he took the key from under the mat and let himself in.

"Summer?" he yelled after locking the front door back up. *She must be upstairs.* He took the stairs two at a time, careful not to shake his camera bag too much. Once he arrived on the second floor, he glanced around at all the progress Summer and her friends had made. The boudoir studio looked amazing. The lavish ivory couch and cream chair complemented the elegant ivory and cream bedding on the massive mahogany bed wonderfully. There was no doubt that all the extra furniture Summer purchased would look wonderful in the boudoir photos that he would take tomorrow, as well as the boudoir photos Aaliyah would take once Bare Sophistication opened for business.

He sat his bag on the floor, noting that the lights were really low in the loft, just as they had been downstairs. The bathroom door was closed, so he assumed she was in there.

He knocked on the door. "Summer, I'll just start setting up."

"Sounds good," she said from the other side of the door. "I'll be right out."

As Aiden walked over to the mirrors and began taking out his camera equipment, he admired more of the studio. He was so proud of everything Summer had accomplished so far, and he couldn't wait to see the enjoyment on her face the day of the grand opening.

The door to the bathroom opened as he was setting up the last of his equipment. "Perfect timing," Aiden said, zipping his camera bag. "Do you have an agenda for tomorrow?"

"I'd much rather talk about tonight."

Aiden stopped what he was doing immediately at the sultry sound in her voice. He glanced up and caught her eyes in the mirror. But it wasn't her eyes that had him hypnotized and speechless at the moment. His gaze raked over her gorgeous legs before noticing a piece of lace peeking from underneath a black satin robe.

"What is this?" he asked, turning around to face her. His voice sounded strained even to his own years.

"This, lover boy, is what I'm calling Seducing Aiden Chase." She dropped the robe, revealing her toned butterscotch body accentuated by purple and black lace and satin lingerie. Sheer black stockings stopped midthigh, and her hair was sexy and free, just like he liked it. Her body was glowing from what he assumed was a combination of shimmer lotion and sexual stimulation. Her stance was so erotic, his entire body tingled with desire and she hadn't even touched him yet.

His eyes were trained to her as she moved across the room and turned on the sound system. Enticing music seeped through the speakers and slapped him right in his groin.

"What are you waiting for?" she asked, sashaying past him toward the bed. "Aren't you going to get your camera?"

Aiden gave her a questioning look. "You want me to take photos of you?"

"Yes," she said, kneeling on the bed and running her fingers through her long curls. "The girls and I talked and we want this boudoir studio to empower women of all ethnic groups, shapes and sizes. It's all about embracing your inner and outer beauty."

She widened her thighs and sank a little farther into the bed. Aiden cleared his throat. "But that's not the only reason I want you to capture this moment." She motioned her finger for him to come closer to her.

"You've been nothing but a gentleman these last few days, but I meant what I said that day we were on the dock. I'm done letting a bad incident define the type of relationship that you and I have. For as long as I can remember, you've been snapping photos of me. Capturing moments and facial expressions that most people don't even know I have."

She took his hand and placed it over her heart. "You've always taken the time to make me feel special. Beautiful. Cherished. Tonight, I want you to capture another moment for me. I almost hadn't realized the limitations I've placed on myself throughout the years, but I see everything clearly now. So tonight, I want you to capture my empowerment. My deliverance from the restrictions I've placed on myself."

She lifted his hand and kissed his palm. "So get your camera…now."

Aiden wasn't sure if it was the authoritative tone in her voice or the way her plush butt looked with a lace panty tucked between its two cheeks. It was probably more the fact that there was never a time in his life that he wouldn't do any- and everything for her. If she wanted him to walk on fire, he'd walk on fire ten times, approach her with burned feet and then ask if she wanted him to do it again.

"Just so we're clear," he said, getting his camera ready. "If at any time you don't feel comfortable, just say the word and this impromptu photo shoot stops."

"I understand, but I doubt we'll stop." She held his gaze and gave him a soft smile before adjusting her position for the first few shots. Within minutes, they'd developed a nice rhythm as he captured pose after pose of Summer's empowerment session. Aiden was in his element, and even though Summer had always impressed him, tonight her perseverance was even more inspiring.

"I'm proud of you," Aiden said, as he put his camera down and pulled her to him. "You were amazing."

"Thank you," she said, returning his hug. But the night wasn't over yet. She had other plans for him that she figured he wouldn't see coming.

"There's only one thing left to do to end this photo shoot."

"What's that?" he asked with a smile. Her eyes dropped to his lips, and instead of responding, she leaned back onto the bed and pulled him down to her. Her lips met his at the same time that his reached for hers. Their kisses weren't hurried, nor were they relaxed. They were demanding at times. Unrushed at other times.

After a few moments, Aiden lifted himself onto his elbows and peered down at her, searching her face. She knew what he was searching for. He wanted to make sure she was okay with whatever happened next. She stared back at him, bold and confident, not hiding the feelings she was sure were reflected in her eyes.

"We may need this," she said slyly, pulling a condom

out of the side of her panties and tossing it on the bed. She read the surprise in his eyes before his mouth curled to the side in a smile.

"I love you, Summer Dupree," he said, brushing a few curls from her face. "Or, rather, I'm in love with you and I have been for a *really* long time."

Summer smiled as she lightly pushed on his chest, ignoring the look of concern on his face. He let her up, looking even more confused when she pushed him back down to the bed and stood in front of him.

She turned so that her butt was facing him as she eased the straps of her bra off her shoulders. She could hear his intake of breath when she tossed the material to the side. Next, she slid her lace panties down her legs, very aware that she'd undressed exactly the same way all those years ago.

"There's the heart," he said in a raspy voice. Summer glanced over her shoulder, down at the birthmark on her butt, before meeting his gaze. She inhaled deeply as she turned so that he could view her body in its entirety. It wasn't shyness that had her taking a deep breath. Quite the contrary. It was the passionate fire in his eyes, exactly what she needed to see. The anticipation almost had her squirming in the spot where she stood.

Still standing, she dipped her mouth to his for a quick kiss before slipping her fingers beneath his shirt. She pushed the fabric up his torso, reaching for his pants next. When she got to his boxers, she slowly inched the fabric down his thighs, amazed by the glorious sight of watching him spring free.

Once they were both naked and protected, she made her way up his body, positioning her core right over his manhood. She looked into his eyes and froze at what she saw. Unlike any of the other times they'd done something sexual, this was the first time nothing was left to question. She knew how Aiden felt about her. She knew he was in love with her. In a way, their friendship had been through hell and back, but now they'd entered a different kind of relationship. They were no longer trying to deny their attraction, but rather embracing the inevitable. Life may be complicated when you fall for your best friend, but a life without a love like that was a worse way to live.

Summer moved her hips slightly on his groin, relishing the amazing way he felt beneath her. He'd given her confirmation, now she needed to return her feelings. "I'm in love with you, too, Aiden Chase," she said, leaning her face closer to his. "And I have been for a *very* long time."

His grin was immediate. He pulled her mouth down to his as she slowly eased herself over his shaft. Inch by inch, she allowed her thighs to spread to accommodate his length. When she was completely locked to his core, they both groaned into each other's mouths. The feeling of him buried deep inside her was all-consuming.

This is the moment I've been waiting for, she thought as she began to move her hips in slow circles. This was the moment that only Aiden could give her. She'd never truly let go during intimacy, even during earlier times she'd shared with Aiden. It wasn't until she thought about her past experiences that she realized that even when they weren't as close, she'd been waiting for the time when they'd reconnect and share the exact moment that they were experiencing now. A time in which they weren't overthinking their relationship but, rather, actually living in the moment.

As feelings and emotions that she'd never felt before began to overtake her body, it brought tears to her eyes.

They'd come such a long way and she knew she'd never love any man as much as she loved the one lying beneath her. Aiden grabbed both cheeks and began to meet her thrusts, arousing more passion from deep within her.

Summer briefly closed her eyes as another wave of sensations rushed through her veins. She could feel him in every part of her body and even though a piece of her wanted to slow down her emotions, she embraced them. She embraced him. She allowed him to take her to a place she'd never gone before. A mind-set that made her feel vulnerable…left her wide open for him to take her any way he wanted. No man ever had a chance with her because it had always been Aiden. He'd always been that one person she couldn't live without. The one person she needed more than she needed her next breath. He consumed her. And instead of being scared by that fact, she felt even more liberated.

Aiden watched Summer's eyes fill with emotion as he tried his best to keep his own feelings under control. Truth be told, he'd always had a difficult time keeping his feelings at bay around Summer, so he knew there was no point trying.

She consumed him, mind, body and soul. Always had. Always would. When he noticed she was on the edge of an orgasm, he increased his speed. He knew it was important for her to remain on top for now, so he held back for as long as he could so she could release her building orgasm.

Then her thighs locked onto his and she thrashed her head back in ecstasy. Her breasts jiggled with every convulsion as her nipples grew even harder. He held her in place, mesmerized by the breathtaking sight before him.

As her spasms subsided, leaving a light sheen of moisture across her body, Aiden swore he'd never witnessed anything more beautiful.

He switched their positions and peered into her eyes, drowning in the love he saw in them. If he could bottle up that look and take it everywhere with him, he would. When it came to the way he felt about Summer, words often couldn't exemplify what he truly felt in his heart.

Even when he'd known that she needed time apart to work through her obstacles, he'd known they would eventually find each other again. They had to. Their once-in-a-lifetime relationship may have changed and matured, but it was still uniquely theirs.

Summer lifted her feet off the bed and wrapped her legs around his waist. He lifted her so that she was in a seated position, which brought him even deeper inside her.

"This feels amazing," she said breathlessly.

"You feel amazing," he whispered into her ear. He felt a building sensation travel from his toes to his thighs. He was close to his own release and every roll of her hips brought him closer to the brink.

Summer must have sensed that he was close, because she adjusted her hips slightly forward, which stimulated the tip of his manhood even more. Within seconds, he succumbed to his own passionate release as he clung to Summer, careful not to hurt her.

She clung to him just as hard, both glistening from the provocative act they'd just performed. She laid her head in the curve of his neck and hugged him even tighter. The last thought Aiden had as he continued to grow, still embedded deep within her, was that he was never letting her walk out of his life again.

Chapter 16

Aiden awoke to rays of sunlight beaming on his face and a peaceful Summer asleep in his arms. *I could get used to this*, he thought as he watched her sleep. Her face glowed like a woman satisfied and he couldn't remember the last time he'd smiled so much.

Being around Summer had always made him smile, but what he was feeling now was different. They were different. They'd both matured a lot over the years and Aiden finally felt as though they were in the exact place they were supposed to be.

He glanced at the digital clock by his bed surprised that it was already 11 a.m. He needed to get out of bed, but he'd contact Danni and let her know that Summer was sleeping in. He didn't want to wake her. He and Summer had stayed up late talking and making love…two of his favorite things to do with her.

A couple days ago, they'd had the photo shoot for Bare Sophistication and Aiden was extremely pleased by the shots he'd taken for his exhibit. He only had a couple more fashion-infused ideas that he wanted to capture through his lens before he'd have all he needed for the exhibit.

Dax had been really thrilled by the preliminary photos he'd seen so far. Last night, Aiden had sent over a few photos of Bare Sophistication pieces that he wanted to include in his exhibit, and any minute now, Dax would be calling to let him know what he thought.

He eased out of bed, careful not to wake Summer, and made his way to his kitchen. He wasn't sure who he would be without her, since she'd been a part of his life for so long. He may have been there for her during some rough times growing up, but she'd been there for him, too. It almost felt like a dream that she was here with him now.

Just after he'd made himself a cup of cinnamon tea, his phone rang.

"Hey, Dax."

"Hey, Aiden. Glad you were available for a quick chat. I loved the photos of Bare Sophistication, and so did the team. We had a conference call this morning with Rogan Studios, including founder Seth Rogan and his team, via Skype. They were really impressed by what they saw and we all agreed that the lingerie photos truly represent the Miami sexiness you're portraying in your exhibit."

"Man, that's great news!" When Dax had told him he was showing some of Aiden's work to Seth Rogan himself, Aiden hadn't really thought much about it. He had been so focused on rebuilding his relationship with Summer at the time.

"It sure is! Right now, you're the top candidate for that position in London. Mr. Rogan was so impressed that he spoke to Palmer Lane and myself. We agreed that you'd be a great featured photographer for a film they're collaborating on in the future."

Hearing Dax mention Rogan Studios and London brought everything back into perspective. He hadn't even told Summer that he was up for a position in London. Deep down, he wasn't even sure he still wanted it.

"That's not all," Dax said. "Mr. Rogan did some research, so he knows your mom is the infamous Mia Meeks. Her travel photography is extremely well-known in London, and it just so happens that Rogan Studios is looking to do a piece on famous parents and their children. His team has already begun reaching out to other artists, musicians and photographers. He'd be interested in discussing that possibility with you further, and since I think you're a shoo-in for that position in London now, I doubt you have anything to worry about."

Aiden sank deeper into his chair and dragged his fingers across his face as Dax continued to talk. For years, he'd been waiting for a better opportunity, and now it had finally fallen in his lap. *Worst timing ever.* Summer was a reasonable person and she wanted him to be happy. He was sure he could talk it over with her and see how it would impact their relationship.

"I'm emailing you a nondisclosure agreement to review right now," Dax said, interrupting his thoughts.

"An agreement for what?"

"Weren't you listening?"

"The phone went out," he lied. "Can you repeat what you said?"

"Sure. I was just saying that Mr. Rogan will be in Miami in two days because he's a guest speaker at a film event near South Beach. In true Seth Rogan fashion, he reserved a yacht for the afternoon and invited us to join him. I assume you can make it."

"Yeah, I can definitely do that."

"Good. I was also saying that all final candidates are requested in London soon for a special project. From what I'm told, even though I think the position is yours, this project carries a lot of weight. His team sent out basic nondisclosure agreements to the five final candidates, so I need you to sign it."

"Sure, but why the rush? When are candidates due to arrive in London?"

"About two and half weeks, the second week of December."

Aiden cringed. Summer's grand opening was also that week. "I can't arrive until after the second weekend in December at the earliest."

"Won't work. I think once you get to London you'll be visiting several different locations. You won't be finished for four to five days after your arrival."

Aiden dragged his fingers over his face once more and groaned louder than he'd meant to.

"What's the deal?" Dax asked.

"Bare Sophistication is having their grand opening that day."

"And you have to be there?"

"I *want* to be there."

Dax was silent for a while. "Listen, Aiden, at first I didn't know why you wanted this job. But now I see it's the position of a lifetime. As your friend and business manager, I think it's too good to pass up. You've been waiting for this point in your life for years."

"I know," Aiden said, taking a sip of his tea. "At first it was all I wanted. Now I'm not so sure."

"I understand. Only you know what the right decision is for you. I just don't want you living with any regrets. So maybe you need to talk to Summer about it. But make it quick. Signed agreements are due back to Rogan Studios' headquarters by 1 p.m. today."

Aiden looked at the clock, noticing it was almost noon. Aiden had to get his thoughts together and he wouldn't be able to do that and talk to Summer about the situation in an hour.

"Is there any clause saying that if you sign the agreement and can't do the secret project, you're out of the running for the position?"

"That's exactly what it says. But there's no harm in signing it if you remove your candidacy for the job."

"Okay, sounds good. Email it to me and I'll sign and scan it back to you. I'll chat with Summer later."

As Dax went over a few more details, Aiden barely listened. All he could think about was that he'd just reconnected with Summer and already he would have to talk to her about the possibility of being gone for a while. Taking the position in London didn't require him to be there 24/7, but it would require him to do a lot of traveling, and he'd probably have to spend at least two weeks at a time there before coming back to the US for two weeks.

That type of lifestyle was hard on solid relationships and even harder on new and developing ones. He definitely had to talk to her before his meeting with Dax and Mr. Rogan. Decisions like this weren't just about him anymore…he and Summer were a unit. *Maybe I should wake her up and talk to her before I sign that agreement.*

When he was almost to his bedroom, his phone rang and an unknown number flashed across the screen.

"Hello, this is Aiden Chase," he said, walking back to the kitchen.

"Aiden, you sound just like your father."

Aiden froze in place.

"Mom?"

"Yes, it's me."

"Is this your new number?"

"Oh, no, sweetie, it isn't. I'm calling from a public phone in Turkey. I just wanted to call you because I got an email from Rogan Studios about a possible documentary."

Damn, they move fast. "Yeah, I just heard about it."

"Good, good. Have you decided to take the position?"

"They told you all of that?"

"Yes, they did. They probably told me so that I could give you some advice."

Advice about what? Mia Meeks wasn't your average mother, and advice wasn't anything she'd ever offered him before.

"Okay, I'm listening."

"Well, for starters, I guess I should be honest in telling you that I haven't booked a big project in a while, so money has been scarce. What you sent me a couple months ago helped, but I need to keep my money flowing and they'll pay us a pretty penny to be a part of this project."

Aiden was silent while he gathered his thoughts. "So the only reason you want to do the documentary is to make money? Not to rebuild our relationship, like you've been telling me for the past two years?"

"Oh, come on, Aiden, you're twisting my words."

"No, I'm not. I'm just saying what you mean, but won't say."

"Baby, I'm honest about the fact that this will help my career. But I also think it will give us a chance to catch up and be a part of something great. You may be closer to your dad, but I'm the parent who understands your drive and determination. I'm the one who understands your artistry. You don't get your talent from your father, you get it from me. It's time for the world to see how great we are when we work together."

"But we've never worked together."

"Exactly. Now's our chance." Noise in the background muffled part of her next sentence. "I have to go, Aiden, I'll talk to you soon. Make the right decision."

After his mom hung up he remained in his kitchen looking out to the ocean. He had a lot of decisions to make and not enough time to make them. One thing he knew for sure was that Summer had enough to handle without having to deal with this, too. He didn't want to sound indecisive when he spoke to her, so he had to figure out what he wanted. Then he'd figure out how to talk to Summer about it.

"Glad you could join us," Seth Rogan said shaking hands with Dax and Aiden. "I know Mr. Perry has informed you about the new developments. We're excited that you've accepted our offer."

Aiden looked at Dax before turning back to Mr. Rogan. He hadn't officially accepted, but Seth Rogan didn't seem to care. When Dax called yesterday morning, he'd told Aiden that he'd been offered the position of vice president of business development for the London office contingent on Aiden's accepting the position of creative director for the merged Palmer Lane and Rogan studios.

Dax had done so much to advance Aiden's career that

he hadn't wanted his friend to lose out on an opportunity, so he'd responded to the email with his encouragement in regard to Dax. But he refused to sign another contract until they met in person.

"Mr. Rogan, although I truly appreciate the offer, what about the secret project that you want candidates to work on?"

"We're still doing that project, but instead of participating, I need you to oversee it. Whoever performs the best will become assistant creative director and report directly to you."

"What about the clause in the contract that says the creative director must live in London for a better part of the year. Is that negotiable?"

"No, unfortunately it won't be negotiable for at least two years." Mr. Rogan carefully observed Aiden. "I'm sure I don't have to remind you how important this merger is to Palmer and I. Ever since we first started our companies, we've considered going into business with one another."

"I understand. It's just that my circumstances have changed since I initially applied for the position."

"Then maybe now is a good time to tell you that we feel as though you have much more experience that we can tap into. It would really bring this endeavor to another level. How does VP of creative sound, working alongside your buddy Daxton Perry?"

Aiden glanced at Dax, who looked nervous about his response. Dax wanted this opportunity. Hell, Aiden didn't know anyone who deserved it more…himself included. But Aiden still hadn't talked to Summer and, quite frankly, he was still a bit torn about his decision. As great as he thought it would be, it wasn't about the job itself. He could take or leave that. It was about the fact that this opportunity would bring him one step closer to working with his mother.

"All of this sounds great, Mr. Rogan, but there's just one thing I don't understand." Aiden crossed an ankle over his knee. "I've been interested in this position for a long time, and although I know my exhibit will be amazing, I've been spotlighted at numerous exhibits in New York and LA. I was even spotlighted in an exhibit in Paris. You and your team didn't seem interested until recently, so why the change of heart?"

"That's simple. You came highly recommended by two people whose opinion I value greatly. After reviewing your profile, I was told separately by both that I'd be stupid not to give you this role. Now, I wasn't really convinced at the time, but after talking to Palmer and Dax, and seeing your work, I'm more convinced that they were right."

"Who were the people whose opinion you valued?"

"Well, your mother for starters. She and I crossed paths many years ago when she was at the peak of her career. Then she had you and stopped taking photos for a while, but we ran into each other in Milan a few months ago. She spent the entire time bragging on you. Understandably, she's really proud of what you've accomplished."

Aiden's jaw twitched. "Are you sure my mother is the woman you talked to?" He could count on the fingers of one hand how many times his mother had actually said she was proud of him. It wasn't that she'd claimed to be disappointed. It was more like she'd never said anything at all, either way.

Mr. Rogan looked confused until he broke out into a

laugh. "Palmer was right. You do have a sarcastic sense of humor. Perfect for Rogan Studios."

"Besides Palmer, Dax and my mother, who was the other person who recommended me?"

Mr. Rogan opened his mouth and was interrupted by the chief steward.

"Come on, fellas," Mr. Rogan said, following the steward. "I have some one-of-a-kind Cuban cigars on the top deck of the yacht. We'll be more comfortable up there."

Aiden reluctantly followed, understanding the decision he had to make about the position the longer he was in the presence of Mr. Rogan. It wasn't that Rogan was a bad man, Aiden just had this strange feeling in the pit of his stomach about the entire opportunity. The sooner he got this meeting over with, the better.

Summer took a step back and did a 360-degree turn in her lingerie boutique. She couldn't believe that Bare Sophistication was opening in two weeks after months of preparing for the grand day.

"Everything is beautiful," Danni said, coming to stand next to her. "Aaliyah and Nicole will be here soon for our meeting. I'll grab us all some coffee and tea before they get here."

Summer nodded her head, but didn't move from her spot after Danni left. She had to soak in the moment. *Danni's right. Everything really is beautiful,* she thought. After such a great week and a half with Aiden, and putting the finishing touches on her shop, life was finally falling into place. There was still a long way to go, but she was confident that not only would her boutique be a success, but her relationship would be, too.

Aiden...

Her mind stayed on him, as it often did. He'd been anxious the past couple days, as if he had something that he wanted to talk to her about, but hadn't. He had a really important work meeting today, but she had a feeling that wasn't the only thing going on. She'd asked him if he needed to talk several times and he'd declined. Just this morning he'd taken a call outside rather than talking in front of her.

It wasn't a big deal, but she'd hoped that after everything they'd been through, he could be completely honest and forthcoming with her. The door opening and closing behind her broke her thoughts.

"That was fast. There must not have been a line." She turned around, expecting to see Danni and froze at the sight before her.

She blinked her eyes a few times, hoping she was in a bad dream and just hadn't awakened yet.

"What the hell are you doing here?" she said with as much force as she could. The intruder didn't seem fazed. In fact, he seemed rather intrigued.

"I always did love when you yelled, angel face," he said with a malicious smile. "Did you miss me?"

Chapter 17

The best revenge is moving on and not giving someone the satisfaction of watching you suffer. No one can make you feel inferior without your consent. Summer thought about the words that were voiced to her by the psychiatrist four years ago. Words that she'd kept tucked deep in a crevice of her mind to reflect on when needed. Today was one of those times.

Staring back at the face of a man who'd robbed her of so much, she realized she had two options. She could back down and let him see her squirm, or she could stand up for herself like she'd wished she'd done years ago.

"You've got a lot of nerve showing up here, Jake."

He glanced around her boutique. "I'd like to think I inspired you a little to open a place like this."

"I don't give you a second thought."

"Funny, because I think about you all the time." She inwardly cringed at his words. He took two steps toward her and she walked behind her counter.

"You need to leave before I call the cops."

"You won't call the cops."

"Yes, I will." She was already reaching for the emergency button under her counter.

"Well, you may want to hear what I have to say first," he said, pulling a laptop out of his briefcase. He opened it, clicked on some buttons, and left it at the edge of the counter. "Better yet, how about you just take a look at my newest business partner." He took a few steps back, but she refused to look at the laptop.

"I could care less about who you're working with."

"I figured you'd say that, but I had to come see you anyway because I had to see the look on your face when I told you. He'd always been too weak to tell you the truth about anything anyway."

Is he talking about Aiden? He can't be...

"I can tell from the look on your face that you assume I'm talking about Aiden, and you'd be correct in that assumption."

The way he was smiling made her nauseous. "What are you talking about?"

Jake sat down in a nearby chair and crossed his arms over his chest. "Why don't you take a look on the laptop?"

Unable to help herself, she quickly walked to the computer, grabbed it and walked back behind the counter.

"Why are you showing me a random website?"

"Just click on the staffing tab and you'll see." She navigated to the staffing page, and the first thing that popped up was a PR announcement that Aiden Chase was the newest VP of creative for the Rogan Studios and Palmer Lane photo and film merger.

Why wouldn't he tell me about this? She skimmed the release before exiting and looking through the rest of the staff, only stopping when she landed on a photo and bio of Jake listed as VP of marketing for Rogan Studios. She closed the laptop and pushed it to the side.

"Seen enough, angel face?"

"I thought I told you to never call me that."

"You liked it." He may have been talking about the pet name, but his words were like a dagger to her heart. A reminder of the night he'd claimed she'd wanted to have sex with him, although he'd drugged her and broken her trust.

Even now, she reminded herself that he hadn't been the first person to break her trust and wouldn't be the last. If Sonia Dupree had prepared her for anything in life, it was that sometimes the people who we thought cared were the first ones to shatter our faith.

Her mind drifted back to Aiden and she wondered again why he hadn't told her about the position.

"He signed a contract," Jake said, waving a sheet of paper at her. Even from a distance, she could tell it was Aiden's signature. "He sent these to my office, too." He rose up from his chair and tossed photos on the counter. She shuffled through a few, noticing that they were all copies of photos Aiden was including in his exhibit.

"Imagine my surprise when I saw the details of the Bare Sophistication photos and noticed the owner was Summer Dupree."

"Why are you showing me all this?"

"I thought it's what you always wanted? For Aiden and I to get along?"

She tried to find any sign of warmth in his eyes and found nothing. "You need to leave before I call the cops."

"What's wrong, Summer? Can't handle the truth? That Aiden was going to move to London and leave you without a second glance?"

She didn't want to ask him to explain, and she shouldn't even be conversing with him, but she was too curious not to ask. "What are you talking about?"

"The job he just accepted is in London."

She tried to mask her surprise, but failed.

"That's right, angel face. Mr. Knight in Shining Armor is leaving for London soon, and from what I've seen on the website for your store, he's leaving right around the grand opening. You may think he cares about you, but what type of man would leave on such an important day?

"Oh, wait, I forgot. Clearly he doesn't care that much if he left you in my hands for five months."

"You despicable son of a..."

"Tsk, tsk, tsk. Careful, angel face. Your claws are showing." He moved his pointer finger back and forth in front of her face.

Summer couldn't place exactly when her frustration hit an all-time high, but before she could rethink her decision, she lifted her hand and smacked him as hard and fast as she could before kneeing him in his genitals the way she'd learned in her self-defense class. Summer ran back to the counter and pressed the alarm, forgetting that her appointment with ADP wasn't until tomorrow morning.

"Who the hell do you think you are?" He lunged toward her, knocking her phone off the counter in the process. It shattered as soon as it hit the ground.

"What's going on?" Danni asked frantically as she dropped the cups of coffee and tea. Jake looked from Summer to Danni before cursing as he grabbed his laptop from the counter and his briefcase.

"Back in college, I thought it would have been much

better," he said, spitting on her floor when he pushed past Danni and walked out the door. "Waste of two years chasing after something that was as forgettable as what I ate for dinner last night. Tell Aiden I'll see him at work, and if you two get married, I'll be sure to give him my condolences for subjecting himself to a life of dissatisfaction."

Summer was still staring at the door after he left.

"Summer, what happened? Who was that?" Danni asked again.

"Did you know that according to the National Institute of Justice, over eighty-five percent of victims who are sexually assaulted in college actually know their attacker?"

Danni looked at Summer in confusion. "What are you saying? What did he do?"

Summer took a deep breath as her eyes remained focused on her front door. She was tired of being quiet. Tired of feeling as though telling her story somehow made her weak, because if there was anything she'd learned over the past month, it was that she was much stronger than she'd ever given herself credit for. On the outside, she'd always held herself with confidence, but she could honestly say that she was now internally confident in her ability to handle any obstacle life threw at her.

"He didn't attack me today, but he assaulted me when we were in college." At Danni's gasp, Summer turned to face her. "I think he showed up here today because he found out Aiden and I were together and he wanted to disrupt my life. I'll tell you more later, but I have to find Aiden and talk to him, first."

Danni studied her eyes before nodding her head in understanding. "I'm here when you're ready to talk. Aaliyah and Nicole should be here soon, too."

"I'll wait to leave until they get here."

"You don't have to," Danni said. "You need to go and find Aiden."

Summer glanced around her shop, well aware of the fact that Jake had purposely sought her out at her workplace to try to disturb her comfort. He wanted her to feel unsafe. It was all a joke to him, and he was trying to make her play the game his way.

"I refuse to give that sick bastard any more power over me. This is my boutique, and tomorrow morning I will walk into the shop and not think about him bursting through here for one second."

"I agree. Do you want to report it?"

Summer glanced at the front door again and thought about how she hadn't reported the assault back in college. At the time, she'd been too embarrassed and afraid that no one would believe what happened when she couldn't even remember what happened herself.

"Yes. I'm calling the cops to report what happened. It probably won't do much good, because the door was unlocked when he walked in, but it's better than nothing."

Danni followed her over to the office phone. "I'll text Aaliyah and Nicole and tell them to bring something much stronger than coffee and tea."

The phone only rang once.

"Nine-one-one. What's your emergency?"

This time, Summer didn't hesitate in her response.

Aiden was well aware that he could get a speeding ticket, the way he was driving, but he had to get to Summer. As soon as the yacht docked, he'd raced to Bare Sophistication, only to find it closed. Then he'd raced to his home only to find all of Summer's stuff gone.

After his calls had gone to voicemail several times, he got hold of Danni, who told him they were at Nicole's place.

He quickly parked his car, hopped out and hit the buzzer. He took the stairs to Nicole's apartment two at a time. Danni was waiting at the door when he got to Nicole's place.

"She's on the balcony. We're going to pick up some food to give you some privacy."

After the ladies left, he found Summer on the balcony with her back toward him. He slid open the door, unsure if she knew he was out there.

"Didn't we just promise each other at the lake a couple weeks ago that we'd be honest about important things from now on?"

"Yes, we did." He leaned on the railing beside her. "I got the voicemail you left on my phone from the main line of the boutique. I was so worried."

"He knocked my phone off the counter and it shattered."

"Why didn't you call the police the minute he arrived?"

"For what?" she asked glancing at him. "For my safety? Or because you're angry that he told me things that you should have told me?"

Her words stung, but they were true. "I was planning on telling you everything. I just couldn't find the right words. There was so much I had to work out and I didn't want to confuse you with my thoughts."

"You could have started with 'Summer, I've accepted a job in London.' That would have worked."

"I didn't accept the actual position, I only accepted the offer to do a special project as part of the competition for the position."

"I'm well aware of Jake's motives, and given his position at the company, I wouldn't be surprised if he added you to the website just to rattle my nerves."

Aiden studied her profile wishing he could embrace her, but knew that it wasn't the right time. "Almost a year ago, I was informed that there would be an opportunity to work in the London office after a merger between Palmer Lane and Rogan Studios. I immediately expressed my interest in the position, and this Miami showcase was key in giving me additional recognition and setting me apart from the competition. On the morning that Dax called me about the contract, my mom called me right after. Apparently, she goes way back with Seth Rogan, and if I accepted the position in London, my mom and I would get an opportunity to be a part of a documentary together."

Summer glanced at him. "Aiden, you know you could have told me that. I know how much you wish you were closer to your mom and I also know how much doing a documentary means to you."

He chanced reaching out for her hand. She didn't pull away. "They also offered my business manager, Dax, the promotion he'd been waiting for, contingent on me taking the position."

"So, basically, they were trying to paint you into a corner by dangling two additional opportunities for two people you care about in your face."

"Pretty much, but I know that's business. Up until now, I've always taken every career opportunity presented to me. Why would they think this would be any different?"

"I guess you're right," she said, looking back out into the sky. "Still doesn't seem right."

"I know, and it got more complicated during my meeting with Seth Rogan and Dax today. Over cigars, I found out that Jake was VP of marketing for Rogan Studios, which you already know due to his unwelcomed visit to your boutique. Apparently, he started with the company eight months ago. Seth Rogan used to be his stepdad, and even though Seth divorced his mom, they maintained a close relationship."

"Yeah, I sort of remembered the story when Jake made me look at the Rogan Studios website. I just hadn't known about the Palmer Lane merger."

"Palmer and Seth go way back. Folks in the photography and film industries know about the merger, but the big announcement won't happen until they complete their team."

As he continued to recount the events from earlier, he noticed that every time Summer glanced his way, her eyes seemed troubled.

"Summer, do you hear what I'm saying? I didn't take that job offer and I'd made that decision before I found out Jake worked for the company."

She sighed. "I heard you. But I don't think you understand why I'm upset with you." She removed her hand from his.

"Then tell me, so I can fix it."

"I don't know if you *can* fix it." She turned to face him. "Aiden, I would never want to stop you from following your dreams, and if taking that job is a dream of yours, then I want you to take it."

"It's not a dream of mine. That's what else I wanted to tell you. I realized that a job with so many contingencies isn't the type of company I want to work for. And I'd never work alongside Jake. It pisses me off just thinking about him walking into Bare Sophistication whenever he pleases."

"How long?" she asked. "How long did you know that you didn't want to take the job in London?"

He looked at her in confusion. "What do you mean?"

"While I was thinking we were taking our relationship to another level. A level that involved a future together. You were unsure about us."

"I was never unsure about us."

"How long did you know you didn't want the job in London?" she asked again. "Honestly think about it."

He observed the determination in her eyes and really thought about his answer before he responded. When he did, he understood why she'd asked. "I knew for sure this afternoon during my meeting."

"Exactly." She averted her eyes before looking back at him. "You may have decided before you knew Jake worked there, but the reason I'm hurt is because after all we've been through…after all the obstacles we've overcome…you still questioned whether you should stay here in Miami with me or take the job in London. And for a few days, you'd chosen London."

He opened his mouth to defend himself but quickly closed it.

"You know I'm right, don't you?" She studied his eyes. "You didn't trust me enough to talk to me so we could work it out together. Then I realized that it's exactly what I did to you all those years ago. I didn't trust you enough to help me work through what I was feeling."

She was the one who reached for *his* hand, then. "Aiden, there is no doubt in my mind that I love you more than I've ever loved anyone in my life. We know each other so well. Almost too well. I know when you're unsure about something, and when I thought back to these past couple of days, I realized all the signs of your uncertainty were there. I had no idea what you were anxious about at first, but now I do. I'm not just angry at you. I'm angry with myself, too."

The way she was looking at him made him feel defeated. He had a sense this conversation wasn't going to go the way he'd planned. "As kids, we used to enjoy the fact that we had running in common. It was something we could bond over. Yet now I realize that we've both been running for so long, sometimes we fall into old habits. Well, I'm done running and I know what I want. I want to ensure that my shop is a success. I want to be more honest with the people in my life about what I'm truly feeling. And, more than anything, I want to be with you. But this time, you're the one who needs some time to work things out."

"No, I don't. I already know that I want to be with you, too."

"In the way that I want to be with you?"

"Yes," he said confidently. "I've always wanted this. I've always wanted us."

She studied his eyes. "Since you're not taking that position in London, what are you going to do?"

"Stay at Palmer Lane here in the US and continue to be a fashion photographer."

"Is that what you want?"

He grew quiet. He really hadn't thought about it. "I'm not sure."

Summer's eyes softened as she moved closer to him. "Aiden, I hope one day you'll understand why I'm saying this, but I think we need some time apart."

"Wasn't eight years enough?"

"We've moved on from that. The reason I say we need some time apart is because you just gave up on a dream you've had for a long time, and I really need you to think about what you want. If you'd told me about London or even asked me how I felt, I would have told you that even if I needed to live with you in London for a while, we would figure it out. I have my store and I'm excited about that, but being with you means I'm willing to make sacrifices, like seeking a partner for the store. I know you love me and would do anything for me, but right now, I want you to focus on you and only you. And I promise that just like you waited eight years for me, I'll be here waiting for you."

Aiden didn't know what to say, but he knew she was right. She knew him better than he knew himself, and even though he didn't want to listen to the words she was saying, he had to acknowledge them whether he liked it or not.

Chapter 18

As much as he reminded himself not to be nervous, he was. It was a beautiful December Miami day, and Aiden had a feeling that luck was on his side. With the exception of the Santa Claus he'd seen running down Ocean Drive in a tight red unitard, white beard and red hat, he hadn't laughed all morning.

There were several scenarios that could come into play today. Scenario 1: Summer could ask him to leave during the opening ceremony. Scenario 2: Summer could let him stay at the grand opening, but avoid him during the after-party. Scenario 3: Since it had been over fourteen days since she had decided that they should take a break, even though they'd still maintained contact, she would be happy to see him and everything would work out as it should.

Lord, please let it be scenario number three. He'd taken her advice because he'd known she was right. But he thought she'd be surprised to know that the decisions regarding his career were the easiest to face.

He'd done a lot of soul-searching these past couple

of weeks, realizing for the first time just how much he'd actually been running. In some ways, reflecting on his actions had reminded him of his mother and the fact that she'd been running most of his life. During those thoughts, he'd felt the most vulnerable. He'd spent so many years chasing a relationship with his mother before he realized that the relationship between a mother and her child was one of the most sacred relationships a person could have. He shouldn't have to chase her. It shouldn't be forced. She should want to have a relationship with him.

Much to his disappointment, he hadn't spoken to her since she expressed her disappointment in him for turning down the creative director position. Even Dax had voiced his understanding when Aiden had explained the situation, so Aiden finally realized what he'd failed to acknowledge for so long. His mother wasn't worth his time. If she ever genuinely expressed interest in repairing their relationship, he would meet her halfway. Until then, he wouldn't hold his breath.

His mind had also ventured to his dad, who had spent almost all of Aiden's time in college and a few years after that in and out of rehab. The most disappointing thing about his relationship with his father was that he couldn't ease the pain his dad had felt upon the death of his own father, followed by his wife leaving him without looking back. He'd visited his dad in New Jersey and they'd had a pretty serious conversation that was over twelve years past due. His dad was even dating a very sweet woman whom Aiden couldn't wait to meet. Reconnecting with his dad had been another important piece of his past that he'd had to address.

By far, though, the most difficult part of his journey

was when he'd flown to Alabama to visit his grandpa Charley's grave site. Grandpa Charley had always been a weak spot for Aiden because he'd loved him so much and he'd never allowed himself to think about a time he wouldn't be around. Being the only grandchild of an only son meant that Aiden's family was extremely small, which also meant that death often made him feel alone in the world. When Grandpa Charley had passed, Aiden had lost a piece of himself. The only person that Grandpa had loved almost as much as he'd loved Aiden was Summer. Now Aiden knew *exactly* what he wanted, and he had to talk to Summer right after her grand opening.

He walked up to the crowd of people gathering in front of the boutique and momentarily lost his train of thought upon seeing Summer. *She's wearing my favorite color.* She looked so beautiful in her formfitting fuchsia dress with her curls free-flowing around her shoulders. He was mesmerized by the way she expertly moved through the crowd with confidence and grace.

Without knowing that he was doing so, he held his breath as she made her way to the part of the audience where he was standing. It seemed like time stood still as her eyes found his in the crowd. There had to be at least fifty people standing around his section on the street, but he only saw her. When she smiled, he felt his lips curl in return, and in true Summer fashion, she made a funny face before waving him over to her.

"I'm so glad you're here," she said, reaching up to hug him.

"Me, too," he said, lifting her into his arms. Aiden had no idea how he'd gone eight years without feeling her embrace when he'd barely been able to go fourteen days.

"Man, I've missed you." He buried his head in the

curve of her neck. "There's no better days than Summer days."

"Well, those are the best days." She giggled just as her name was being called. "Come on up to the front and stand with the family and friends. I have to cut the ribbon soon."

As he followed her to the storefront, he smiled as he looked up to the clouds and kissed two fingers to the air. *No doubt you're guiding me through this, Grandpa Charley.* He had his own angel fighting for his love. Now all he had to do was get through the day so that he could talk to her.

"Guys, you're going to make me cry," Danni said waving a hand in front of her face. "Are you serious?"

Summer glanced at Winter and Autumn before turning back to Danni. "We couldn't be more serious. You've been such an integral part of the success of the Bare Sophistication platform. It only seems fitting that you be a partner."

The opening of Bare Sophistication lingerie boutique and boudoir studio had been a huge success, and Aaliyah and Nicole had just informed her that they'd received boudoir bookings through the summer of the following year. Their women's empowerment message seemed to really resonate with the women of Miami, and Summer couldn't wait to see what the future had in store for the shop.

Everything had gone off without a hitch, and now only her friends and family remained in the store enjoying the grand opening after-party.

"You're more than deserving of this," Winter said, giving Danni a hug as tears began to fall. She was already going on five months pregnant and her hormones were at an all-time high. Summer had lost count of how many times Winter had cried today.

Last week, Danni had informed Summer that she wanted to ask Winter and Autumn if it would be okay for her to keep her full-time role in Miami. When she'd initially mentioned it, Summer realized that she'd forgotten that Danni was only temporarily in Miami. She'd grown so close to Danni, and after telling her how much she'd love it if Danni stayed, Summer had spoken to Winter and Autumn. She mentioned the idea of possibly making Danni a partner, and her sisters had wholeheartedly agreed that they couldn't imagine Bare Sophistication without Danni.

"I hate to break up the lovefest," Autumn said, glancing over her shoulder. "But there's a man who's been waiting patiently all day to talk to a very special someone."

Summer followed the direction her sister was looking in and her eyes instantly landed on Aiden, who was talking to her brother-in-law. He looked so good in his sea green jeans, white T-shirt, and cream blazer. She'd always loved how he looked in blue or green. Actually, she loved how he looked in almost any color. As usual, only Aiden could take a simple outfit and make it look so flawless.

"You should go talk to him," Danni said, nodding in Aiden's direction. "He really has been waiting all day."

They were right. He'd pitched in to help throughout, and even though he hadn't tried to pull her aside—unless it was to make sure she wasn't overwhelmed—she knew he wanted to talk to her.

"I'll be back," she said, giving her sisters and Danni a smile.

"I doubt it," Danni said, smiling back.

Aiden held her gaze the entire time she walked toward him. She wasn't even sure when her brother-in-law had walked away, because her eyes had been fixed on Aiden.

"Today went extremely well," he said when she stopped in front of him. "I'm so proud of you and I hope you're just as proud of yourself."

"I am. I couldn't have asked for a better grand opening."

His eyes studied hers and she could tell he had much more to say. "Can you follow me somewhere?"

"It's dark out," she said with a laugh.

"You can't walk outside in the dark?"

"It's not that." She glanced around her boutique to see how many people were left at the after-party. "How can I leave my own grand opening?"

"I'll show you," Aiden said, standing on a nearby chair. "Attention, family and friends," he said, yelling over the music. "Would anyone mind if I steal Summer for a while?"

"Nope," Winter yelled from the other side of the room. "Keep her for as long as you want."

"I'll lock up," Danni yelled after.

"Great." Aiden got down from the chair and extended his arm to her. "Care to join me now?"

She laughed at his bold antics. He was always doing things to surprise her. "Sure."

As they walked to a destination that she wasn't sure of, she tried to slow the butterflies in her stomach. She wasn't even certain why she was nervous, but Aiden seemed to have that effect on her.

"Only you could make an announcement to my family that you needed to steal me away and get a response to keep me for as long as you wanted. I honestly think my family loves you more than me sometimes."

"You're just realizing that," he said with a laugh. "I knew they wanted to replace you with me about two decades ago. You're late."

She punched him in the arm and he pretended that it hurt. They slowed their walk as they approached a building that was a couple of blocks from hers.

"Where are we?"

"You'll see." He led her into the darkened building and locked the front door.

"Do you remember when you asked me what I wanted to do with my career since I hadn't taken that job, and I told you I wasn't sure?"

"Of course I remember."

"Well, I finally figured out what I wanted to do. And before you asked, no, I didn't decide to stay at Palmer Lane."

"You didn't?"

"Nope. After everything that happened, I realized that I'd only remained at Palmer Lane for so long because I was comfortable there, and being employed at the company was the only consistent part of my life. So I thought long and hard about my next steps, daring myself to revisit my high school days when I'd had so many dreams about where I'd be by now."

He walked her to a spot in the middle of the darkened room and asked her to stand there while he turned on the lights.

"After days of perfecting my business plan, I finally got all the puzzle pieces lined up in the correct places.

Now all I need to do is put the pieces together and finalize the details. So tonight, I'd like to present to you Aiden Chase Artistry."

The minute he turned on the lights, Summer gasped in surprise. Not only did she immediately notice that the photos and art on the walls were a combination of old and new pieces that Aiden had painted or photographed, but she noticed that every image and every painting had something to do with her.

She spun in a slow circle, noticing that even two of the images he'd taken that night in her boutique were on the wall, but they were beautiful shots with her back turned toward the camera. On one photo, the words *dare to empower* were in the bottom corner and the other was inscribed with *beautiful liberation*.

"You're opening your own studio," she said as a comment rather than a question.

"Yes, I am. I plan on having the grand opening at the beginning of March to give me time to iron out all the details. And I'm not just opening this studio to display my work. I'm also going to be giving photography and painting classes. I'm officially in business for myself, and with Dax's help, I've already landed several large photo shoots in the US and overseas as an independent contractor."

"That's so great, Aiden. Is Dax still with Palmer Lane?"

"He is, but he refuses to work for Rogan Studios. Palmer Lane is a good company, and when Palmer heard about the ultimatum I was given, Dax ended up getting a similar promotion in the New York office. Palmer and Rogan still have the business venture in London, but this move is best for Dax. He's happy and we're still friends."

She walked to the back of the studio, noticing that the images and paintings weren't all recent work. Some of the photos of her dated back to childhood. "I'm so proud of you."

"Thank you." He walked over to where she was standing and stopped right beside her. "Did I mention that I was in Chicago last week on an important visit with Malik and Micah, along with Micah's business partner, Shawn Miles?"

"No one told me. Why were you there?" Her cousin Micah used to be a police officer, and now he co-owned M&M Security Firm in Chicago. Shawn and Malik had formerly worked in the FBI together, and now Malik was a private investigator and Micah had teamed up with Shawn to open the security firm.

"I reached out to them as soon as I learned Jake worked for Rogan Studios. I hadn't done anything eight years ago, but I refused to let him get away with what I'd suspected he'd done to other women. I didn't tell Malik or Micah why I needed them to find out info on Jake, but I did tell them it had something to do with you. It's possible that they put two and two together, because last week, I flew down to meet them after they uncovered information."

"What did they find out?"

"That you weren't his only victim. There had been several cases thrown out when he was in high school. Seth Rogan had a lot of connections in law enforcement. There was also one case that Malik said Mr. Rogan had tried to have hidden, but he was able to uncover it. Apparently, three years ago Jake's ex-girlfriend had reported that he not only sexually assaulted her while she was asleep, but she found DVDs of seven additional incidents. He must have been drugging her because she didn't know. He slipped up the last time and didn't give her as strong of a dosage. She reported it as soon as she figured it out, but the case went nowhere."

Summer shut her eyes as she tried to keep her anger at bay. "I've never wished ill on anyone, but that man brings me to the brink of an anger I've never felt before. It makes me sick to my stomach to think that even when women do the right thing and report an assault, it's still our word against his."

"I know," he said pulling her to him. "But now the right folks know what happened and his ex-girlfriend has been contacted. Nothing will probably happen to Seth Rogan for paying to have the cases covered up. Unfortunately, with men like that, those who do the dirty work are the ones who pay. However, Jake will pay for what he's done. Law enforcement is already handling it, and if that wasn't enough, your cousins and I may or may not have paid him a visit."

"Did you threaten him?"

He gave her a sly smile. "Define *threaten*."

"You know what threaten means."

"Let's just say I did something I should have done a long time ago."

"Okay," she said, knowing he probably wouldn't tell her more than that. Her eyes widened in realization. "Now I understand why Malik and Micah have been randomly calling and texting me. You're right, they must have put two and two together."

"Probably." Aiden began rubbing small circles along her spine with his thumb. She looked up at him before returning her attention to the images on the wall.

"Are you going to tell me why there are so many images of me in your studio?"

"I decided that I'll change the exhibit every three months, with the exception of my favorite photos, which may be on permanent display. For my grand opening, I wanted it to be about me."

She looked at him in confusion. "But every piece in here is me."

"Exactly." He leaned in and placed a sweet kiss on her lips. "I'm displaying pieces that encourage and motivate me to be a better man. Pieces that, through every facet of my life, have helped me overcome some difficult obstacles and kept me company when I felt lonely."

Her heartbeat quickened as Aiden led her to one of the first pictures he'd ever taken of her. She had to be no older than ten.

"This exhibit is about the very person who has impacted my life so profoundly that I can't imagine what type of man I'd be if it weren't for the inspiration she instills in me. Summer, for as long as I can remember, you have been the one piece in my puzzle that has always remained unchanging. Even when we took a break and didn't communicate that often, you were always right were you belonged." He took one of her hands and placed it over his chest. "You were always right there in my heart."

His words touched her deep in her core, evoking emotions that only Aiden could induce.

"This exhibit is called *There Are No Better Days than Summer Days* because I would not be the man I am today if it weren't for you. I truly believe that. And what I've realized over the past couple of months is that dating you is the furthest thing from my mind. When people date, it's to get to know one another with the hopes of finding commonality and falling in love. We've been there, done that and quite frankly, dating you just isn't enough for me."

She almost felt like she was in a daydream when he knelt in front of her and pulled out a gorgeous diamond ring. "Summer Dupree, will you do me the honor of being my wife…my everything?"

Summer gazed into his eyes, filled with more passion than she ever thought possible. "Aiden Chase, I've loved you since before I truly knew what love was. There's no reason to date when the man you're meant to spend the rest of your life with steals your heart in kindergarten. I love you unconditionally, so the answer is yes, I will marry you."

Aiden's lips curled into that sexy side smile before turning into a full-blown grin. He stood after placing the ring on her finger and pulled her into a loving kiss filled with passionate promise. Summer was so wrapped up in the moment, she didn't hear the knocks on the window until Aiden broke the kiss. She glanced over at all her family and friends standing by the door waiting to come in.

"Everyone knew you were going to propose?"

"Of course," he said with a laugh. "They're like family to me, too, and I needed Danni, Nicole and Aaliyah's help getting this place together."

"You never cease to amaze me," she said, giving him another quick kiss. "What if I had said no?"

Aiden gave her a wicked smile. "Then I'd have to use my charming persuasion to win you over."

She laughed as they walked to the front door. She definitely didn't need to know how that would have gone. If there was anyone who knew how persuasive Aiden was, it was her. He'd been reeling her in ever since she was five years old, and she had a feeling he'd continue making her fall even deeper in love as time went on.

Epilogue

Six months later...

Aiden adjusted the collar of his tux for the fifth time as he stood in the courtyard of Deering Estate along the edge of Biscayne Bay in Miami. As much as he reminded himself not to be nervous, he couldn't help it.

The moment he'd proposed to Summer, he'd been counting down to his wedding day. He was glad that Summer had agreed to get married in six short months rather than a year. They'd already started their life together, but he was ready to officially be husband and wife.

After they'd purchased a house not far from the town house he'd rented, she accompanied him to the Middle East on his first photo shoot as an independent contractor, and since then, they'd taken several more trips together.

After six months, they'd developed a healthy work-life balance and Aiden honestly couldn't remember the last time he'd been so happy.

"Don't be nervous," Malakai whispered to him. "You and Summer are ready for this moment."

"Thanks, man." Aiden was fortunate that he'd been able to further reconnect with Summer's sisters and cousins through the course of their engagement. He'd always imagined that if he married Summer, Malakai would be his best man. Now he actually was.

Aiden briefly looked at his dad, who was sitting in the front row with his girlfriend. His mother had decided not to come and he wasn't the least bit surprised. Aiden definitely respected all the single moms raising their children without the help of the fathers. But thinking about his dad and Summer's dad, who was in attendance as well, he couldn't help but appreciate the single fathers raising their children without the help of the mothers.

Aiden glanced to the sky and took a deep breath. He was sure Grandpa Charley was smiling down at him. Just then, the music began indicating that the wedding party would be walking down the aisle soon. When the music changed and he got a glimpse of Summer in a stunning white gown, everything drowned out around him.

She was breathtaking. Mesmerizing. Beautiful inside and out. Aiden wasn't the type to cry and couldn't remember the last time he'd felt so much emotion. Yet today, he had to briefly shut his eyes from the onslaught of feelings running through his body as he watched Summer walk down the aisle. When her father handed her over to him and she slipped her hand in his, he had to force himself not to kiss her right then and there. Most of the first part of their ceremony was a blur, until Aiden heard the officiant announce that they'd chosen to say their own vows. Aiden was asked to share his first.

"Summer, I thought long and hard about what I would

say to you—the woman I've loved for most of my life. I thought about standing up here and promising to always leave the toilet seat down, to always take out the trash before it overflows and to always fix things in the house when they break. But then I realized that there will be times when I leave the toilet seat up. I'll be sure to take out the trash, but it may overflow at times. And you and I both know that I'm crafty with my hands, but it takes me days to fix things, so that wouldn't be a fair promise."

Summer smiled and everyone laughed. "The more I thought about my vows, the more I realized that all I needed to do was say what's truly in my heart. There were so many hurdles we had to overcome to get to this moment. So many times I thought I'd never get married because I couldn't get married to anyone who wasn't Summer Dupree. My best friend. The woman who knows me better than I know myself." He felt the tears in the back of his eyes sneaking up to the surface the longer he looked at Summer.

"Summer, I love you with every part of my soul. Every piece of my mind and inch of my being belongs to you. It always has. It always will. To love someone—and I mean to truly love someone more than you love yourself—for over twenty-five years is a testimony that I've lived. It's a testimony that I'm still living. You've *always* had my heart and today—on this absolute perfect day—I'm finally marrying the woman of my dreams and future mother of my children. I've told you this before and I'll tell you this every day of our lives. When I look in the mirror at the reflection staring back at me, there isn't a part of me that I see that doesn't have you in it. I promise to always support your dreams. I promise to respect our differences and to always be open and honest with you. And I promise to love you unconditionally…for the rest of my life."

By the end of his vows, tears rimmed the edges of her eyes, causing the tears he'd been blinking back to fall down his cheeks. Summer briefly released one hand to rub the locket he'd given her over twenty years ago. One hundred guests were in attendance and Aiden could only see her. He doubted it would ever be any other way.

Summer wasn't sure she could get through her vows without crying. Especially seeing Aiden so emotional over his. When the officiant cued her to go, she took a deep breath before speaking.

"What do you say to a man who's been such an instrumental person in your life? How do you tell the man you love and have loved ever since you were a child that he's the reason you're a better woman? He's the reason you can stand before one hundred people with the confidence to say that life has thrown me some massive curveballs, but I survived every one by rising above them.

"Aiden, you've been my best friend and fiercest protector throughout my entire life. When I was nine, you gave me the locket I'm wearing now and you told me that every time I felt alone and needed to escape, to look at it and know that you're right there with me. I can't tell you how many times I've looked at this locket throughout the years. Even when we were apart, I knew you had my back, and as long as I remembered that, everything in the world was okay."

She swallowed back her emotion when he lightly squeezed her hand. "Through all the obstacles we've had to face, we stand before one another today unbroken. We learned at an early age that we are much stronger together than we are apart, and there isn't a day that goes by that I don't thank God for blessing me with an amazing man like you. I promise to always stand beside you in struggle. Laugh during all the good times. Take care of you in any and every way you need it. Today, and every day hereafter, I promise to trust and love you with all my heart and soul. We solidified our bond in kindergarten and now, over twenty-five years later, we'll solidify an even stronger dedication to one another, and I can't wait to share the rest of our lives together."

By the time Summer had finished her vows, there wasn't a dry eye in the audience. She'd waited her entire life for this moment with Aiden, and she knew he'd waited just as long. Standing there, finally being able to kiss her husband and the man she loved more than life itself, she was overcome with a wave of completion. Loving someone was easy, but giving yourself to someone without reservation was the best feeling in the world.

"There are no better days than summer days and I'd wait another thirty years if it meant I'd get to eventually have this moment with you," Aiden whispered to her as they were announced as Mr. and Mrs. Chase. She smiled before pulling him in for another deep kiss. *I'd wait even longer*, she thought. One thing she knew for sure… *This* moment was well worth the wait.

* * * * *

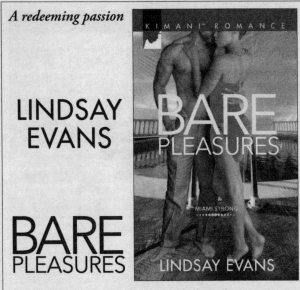

REQUEST YOUR FREE BOOKS!

2 FREE NOVELS PLUS 2 FREE GIFTS!

KIMANI™
ROMANCE

Love's ultimate destination!

SPECIAL EXCERPT FROM

*Everything schoolteacher Morgan Hill loves is in her
hometown of Temptation, Virginia—her twins,
her students and the charming community center
where she's staging their holiday play. But now the
building's new owner, Grayson Taylor, is putting sexy
visions into Morgan's head, making the young widow
long for a future even Santa couldn't deliver...*

*Read on for a sneak peek at
ONE MISTLETOE WISH,
the first exciting installment in author A.C. Arthur's
TAYLORS OF TEMPTATION series!*

Her back was to the window and Gray moved to stand
in front of her. He rubbed the backs of his fingers lightly
over her cheek.

"Those buildings mean something to you, don't they?"
he asked her.

She shrugged, shifting from one foot to the other as if
his proximity was making her nervous. Being this close
to her was making him hot and aroused. He wondered if
that was what she was really feeling, as well.

"This town means something to me. There are good
people here and we're trying to do good things."

KPEXP1116

"That's what my mother used to say," Gray continued, loving the feel of her smooth skin beneath his touch. "Temptation was a good place. Love, family, loyalty. They meant something to the town. Always. That's what she used to tell us when we were young. But that was after the show, after my father found something better outside of this precious town of Temptation."

Gray could hear the sting to his tone, felt the tensing of his muscles that came each time he thought about Theodor Taylor and all that he'd done to his family. Yes, Gray had buried his father two months ago. He'd followed the old man's wishes right down to the ornate gold handles on the slate-gray casket, but Gray still hated him. He still despised any man that could walk away from his family without ever looking back.

"Show me something better," he found himself saying as he stared down into Morgan's light brown eyes. "Show me what this town is really about and maybe I'll reconsider selling."

"Are you making a bargain with me?" she asked. "Because if you are, I don't know what to say. I'm not used to wheeling and dealing big businessmen like you."

"I'm asking you to give me a reason why I shouldn't sell those buildings. Just one will do. If you can convince me—"

She was already shaking her head. "I won't sleep with you, if that's what you mean by *convince* you."

Don't miss ONE MISTLETOE WISH
by A.C. Arthur, available December 2016
wherever Harlequin® Kimani Romance™
books and ebooks are sold.